ARTICLE 58

Russell John Connor

Article 58

Published June 2014 by emp3books Ltd
Norwood House, Elvetham Road, Fleet, GU51 4HL

Printed and Bound by Lightning Source.

Set in Bookman Old Style. Front cover graphic bought under licence from Getty Images.

Illustrated by Tenija Kornhubere.

Printed on acid-free paper from managed forests. This book is printed on demand, so no copies will be remaindered or pulped.

ISBN 978-1-907140-91-4

Dedicated to The Children of Siberia

Article 58

Man is a creature that can get used to anything, and I think that this is the best definition of him.

Fyodor Dostoevsky
House of the Dead

Article 58

Contents

Preface

In June 1941 tens of thousands of people from the Baltic region were deported following the occupation and annexation of the Baltic states by the Soviet Union. The procedure for deporting the 'enemies of the people', as defined under Article 58 of the Soviet penal code, was issued by Ivan Serov in the so-called Serov Instructions*. Under the supervision of the NKVD (the forerunner of the KGB), men were generally imprisoned and most of them died in Siberian gulags. Women and children were resettled in Kirov, Tomsk, Omsk and Novosibirsk Oblast and Krasnoyarsk as well as further north in Igarka. About a half of them survived.

* See Appendix

Article 58

March 8th 1953

Walking past the window of a shabby looking hotel Janis glimpsed his reflection. He thought that he looked old for his years. His fur hat covered his grey hair but his limp promoted the impression that he was close to pension age. Janis had to remind himself that he was only twenty seven. Glancing at his wife by his side, he thought, 'Hilkka looks more beautiful than ever.'

Janis and Hilkka entered the hotel and rang a bell to attract attention. After a long wait a panel in the wall above a small desk clattered open and a face peered out dominated by a grey bushy beard. Janis asked the beard whether a room was available for two nights, and he fully expected the answer to be 'no'. Judging by how crowded the train was upon which they recently arrived into Moscow and the amount of people they had seen pouring into the city, they thought that all accommodation must, by now, be full.

The beard looked the couple up and down and then demanded, 'Documents.' Janis handed over their passports and a typed letter stating that he had been permitted to return to Siberia in voluntary exile. The beard studied the papers. If there was any quizzical thought as to whether there is such a thing as 'voluntary exile', nothing was expressed. His only words were a half grunted, 'Eleven roubles each night

3

– up front.' Janis was pleasantly surprised that there was a room but had to make a quick mental calculation to see if they could afford this. Their onward train had been delayed for two days and he had not anticipated paying for hotels. Understanding anyway that there was no alternative, Janis duly paid the money and, together with Hilkka, he made his way up two flights of thinly carpeted stairs.

Janis and Hilkka looked at each other as they entered the room. Although small and sparsely furnished, it was tidy and the sheets looked clean. The black painted wood flooring was partially covered by a green and brown patterned rug. There were two single beds covered with knitted quilts that were positioned, bizarrely, on either side of the room.

This was the first hotel that the couple had been in and they both felt quite excited.

Heated by large old radiators, which were working at their maximum, the room was oppressively hot. Janis opened the double window to let in some cold air and noticed that wet snow had started to fall. Opposite, he could see large puddles of sludgy water were waiting for speedy motorists to make the sad looking pedestrians and people queuing for a bus even more unhappy as they hurled freezing water at their legs. 'Moscow is a depressing city,' he remarked to Hilkka.

Janis could see the railway station in the distance and the crowds that continued to flow from it. He noticed that the trams heading towards the centre were also full. Shutting out the icy draught Janis said to Hilkka, 'It's like Uncle Joe has created such a

4

vacuum that he's sucking in people from all corners of the Empire.' He mused for a short while on what he had just said. A few days before, he would never have referred to Stalin as Uncle Joe, even in private to Hilkka.

The couple, luxuriating in the space of their small hotel room, took off their heavy winter coats and hats, unpacked their few belongings and laid them out on one of the beds. Hilkka put her spare underwear and presents for her sisters in one of the drawers of the small chest.

Compared to their planned onward journey, it had been a relatively short trip from Riga but as all the sleeping compartments were booked, Janis and Hilkka snatched what sleep they could on the hard wooden benches in their seated carriage. However, as the train approached Moscow it became crowded and they spent the last five hours crushed against each other, squashed in by a mass whose intent was to take a last glimpse of their leader who lay cold in the House of Unions.

It was late in the morning but Janis and Hilkka decided to catch up with their sleep.

Janis poured two Russian sized measures of Rigas Balsams that they had brought with them together with two glasses and gave one to Hilkka. The both drank, looked at each other and Janis said, 'To our future, to our new life.' It was as if Hilkka had drunk a sleeping draught, as she lay back on the bed and closed her eyes.

Janis sat on the edge of the bed for a while and let the combination of balsams and the warm room take effect. Turning to Hilkka he looked at her. He thought that with her round face and blonde hair she was as angelic as the first time that he had woken from his coma and seen her. Then he looked along her slender body and began to stroke her leg. He noticed that it became warmer as he moved up. Slowly, he unbuttoned her black blouse and touched the necklace that once belonged to his mother before running his finger just under the top of her bra-strap. Hilkka opened her eyes and said, 'Kiss me.'

Janis lent forward and kissed his wife and then pulled back slightly to take in her whole face. He saw the gleam in her eye that he thought had been extinguished forever. Janis felt that a heavy weight had been lifted from his shoulders.

Maybe because they were returning to where they got married, Janis thought of their first dance together on their wedding night. 'Do you remember our first waltz?' he asked and added, 'may I have this one?' Gently and sensuously their bodies moved easily together. Hilkka was very light and graciously let him lead. He could feel the blood rising. Entwining each other, their hands ran to an easy rhythm, exploring, opening, caressing. Slow, quick, quick, slow gave way to a more urgent beat. The hips swayed and the fire rose from below.

Two bodies moved in unison, responding, sensuous and arched. Hilkka pressured herself onto his urgent and needy tongue. 'Jani'. The way she shortened his name heightened his desire to possess her completely.

Hilkka's short sharp breath and deep muscular twitches made him quicken his attentions.

Time stopped. There was a mini death as if two dancers had come to their spectacular end and now nothing mattered.

Janis remained in Hilkka for as long as his poor retreating body let him. 'Say me something,' Hilkka asked. When he did not immediately answer she said, 'I love you'. Janis replied, 'And I love you too.' He had never been more certain of anything.

Hilkka asked 'Do you really love me?' Depression seemed to follow the heights as night follows day.

Janis heard Hilkka's breathing change to that of a deeper and throatier sound and he was left alone to think. He was prepared to go to sleep but sleep did not overtake him.

Thoughts turned to being in Moscow at this strange time. To Janis the whole country seemed to be in a state of shock. Any conversation that he overheard related to how would they cope without the great man. 'Was this the same great man,' he thought, 'who had ordered our deportation? Was this the same great man who classified me as a child of an enemy of the people and nearly froze us to death? Was this the same great man who made me into an informer and a real enemy of the people?'

Sleep still would not come and Janis' thoughts returned to his childhood. He remembered the time that he had been a patient in the main hospital in

Riga, Latvia. It was late spring in 1940. He had glandular fever and had spent six weeks being cared for. When he was convalescing he took an active interest in the work of the doctors and had decided then that medicine would be his future career. 'My wishes came true', Janis thought ironically, 'what a great job I had as a general hand.'

Janis remembered the time he had spent in a general ward together with a rich variety of patients. A chess champion was in the next bed and opposite him was a dockworker and then a company director replaced him. It was at the time of the Soviet-Finnish war and there were good-natured debates about politics. Everyone had been on the side of the brave Finns that were holding out against the Soviet aggression. Janis mused on the forces of fate and destiny that had fused Hilkka and himself together in the far north of Siberia and pondered, 'Could I ever have imagined that at the same time that I was in hospital my future wife was being forcibly removed from her home in Finland?'

In hospital Janis had listened in to the news about Polish soldiers being interned on Latvian soil but war in his country had seemed such a distant possibility. He was more interested in the process of checking and monitoring that was carried out on the ward and the machine that could see through Mr. Laukman's chest.

Two months later the Red Army marched into Riga.

Janis' thoughts turned to the day when his mother returned in tears from a song festival. Soon after, his father came back unexpectedly early from his office. Janis heard them say, 'So much for remaining in your place, I will remain in mine.' He knew they were referring to a recent speech by the President. On the same day, around five in the evening, an armoured car stopped in the street opposite Janis' bedroom window. He watched as the gun turret turned menacingly around. Having shown itself the car eventually moved off. Janis wanted to run to warn his friend who lived a few streets down but his mother refused to allow him to go out.

Janis thought about the journey ahead and the reunion that awaited him. He wondered how his mother would look now. It was seven years since he had last seen her and he knew that Siberia took its toll on the body and soul. 'One year out there must be equivalent to three anywhere else', he thought. Then he suspected that she would look rather well as she had survived all that had been thrown at her in those early years. 'How did she manage?' he pondered. He thought about his mother's background, 'She was the daughter of a wealthy Russian merchant and then a high society wife and devoted mother. What could have prepared her for the hardship to come and how did she survive when so many did not?' The answer was not clear to Janis at all.

Janis resigned himself to not catching up with his missing sleep. He listened to his wife's breathing and thought, 'Here I am lying by the woman that I love. I wouldn't be here now if I hadn't gone to Siberia or if I'd stayed in Riga and been conscripted into the German or Russian armies. I am a lucky man.'

As the hours passed, Janis began to think of the journey that he and Hilkka were about to undertake and the one that he and his mother had endured over a decade earlier.

June 14th 1941

The sun had just risen and was gleaming in through the bedroom window when a loud thumping on the door and shouts of '*Otkroite* – open up,' suddenly awakened Janis. 'When had anyone banged on the door like that?' he thought. Hesitantly he got out of bed, put his dressing gown on, and went downstairs. To his surprise, his parents were already there and his father opened the door. 'Had they been expecting whoever was knocking at such an early hour?' Janis thought quizzically.

Three men came into the room. The first one, who was clearly the leader, wore a greyish brown coat, which seemed far too heavy for such a warm summer's night. A local policeman followed him. The third was a Russian Army officer. Janis knew that he was army and not NKVD because the NKVD wore blue caps with a red trim.

The leader ordered Janis and his parents to sit with their hands on the big table in the dining room whilst the army officer began to search the house. 'Declare now, if you have any weapons,' the leader boomed in Latvian with a heavy Russian accent. Janis surmised that this man must have once lived in his country and had returned with the occupation.

The leader addressed Janis' father, 'Reinis Mednis. Under Article 58, you are an enemy of the people. Now

11

you and your family have one hour to pack all belongings you can carry by hand.' Janis was shocked, not so much by the entry of these three men or the order to pack but by the term 'enemy of the people'. He was proud of his father's past as a patriot and fighter in the Latvian Riflemen and now as the Chief Chemical Engineer at Shell. 'Surely there must be a mistake here?' Janis thought. The leader spat out a series of questions at his father, 'Who are you working for? How did you come to be a spy? Who recruited you?' Janis did not realise it at the time but he was to hear again and again these same questions - later directed at him.

Janis and his mother were ordered to gather their belongings whilst his father had to remain with his hands on the table. His father said, 'Sonja, do as the man says,' and was then rebuked for talking without permission. When he could, Janis whispered to his mother, 'What about Ginta?' Ginta, his older sister, happened to be staying with friends outside of Riga. Sonja put her finger to her lips and nothing more was mentioned. Hurriedly they packed suitcases and at the last minute Janis threw into one a harmonica that he had been given for his name day. He decided that his savings book with forty lats in it could be left. Then they were ordered down the communal stairs of their apartment block and into the street. Canvas-covered trucks waited for them there. Janis looked along Alberts Street. The tall and elegant houses were so familiar but this scene seemed so unreal. The plaster figures of the art nouveau facades looked on and it seemed to him that even the plaster faces were in shock.

Janis and his parents climbed into the trucks to find forlorn families already sitting there. He knew two of them. They were Jews who owned the local stores. They all had been sitting in the truck for a few minutes when the army officer threw in a bundle of clothes including a uniform he had found in a cupboard together with a set of skis. 'These will come in useful,' the officer grunted. Little did Janis know then that these last few items would save their lives later in the year.

The street was deserted when the trucks rumbled away over the cobbles towards the railway station. It was still only four thirty in the morning. When they arrived at the station the men were ordered out of the trucks. Janis' father rose, looked at his son, took him by the hand and said in a strong, steady voice, 'Be brave and look after Mamma.' He then kissed his wife, said, 'Sonja my love, be strong,' and stepped down to be confronted by two small Soviet soldiers with bayonets fixed on their rifles. Janis thought how smart his father looked with his straight back and his polished Latvian Rifleman boots. He clutched the pocketknife just handed to him, which still held the warmth of his father's hand. The men's silhouettes disappeared into the bright early morning sunshine that gleamed off the tangle of railway lines. Disappeared forever.

The rest of the group, which now consisted of women and children, were driven a short distance and they stopped opposite a dark green freight car, the sort that was often seen transporting cattle. The door was open and from inside the darkness came the sound of hysterical crying. A young woman sat with her small baby, utterly forlorn, next to a small suitcase and a half-filled basket.

The freight car had been modified to include rough looking bunks and a hole in the floor, which Janis hoped wasn't for the use he first thought of. He and

14

his mother were ushered on and they sat in a corner on the hard, rough planks without even hay that cattle might have been given. Quickly the car filled up and eventually contained thirty-two people. Janis had nothing else to do other than count and recount to make sure he had the number right. The train did not move for a long while and gradually a crowd gathered with people calling to find friends and relatives. Janis kept an ear out for voices that he recognised and clung to the shred of hope that he and his family might be reprieved at the last moment. To his growing distress, no friendly voice shouted out, 'Stop, you have the wrong family.'

Accompanied by crying and shouts of anguish from the distraught crowd, the doors of the freight cars were slammed shut. The engine's whistle blew and it sounded like a cry for help for the unhappy load, which it was destined to lead into an unknown future. The train jerked and clattered as the huge steam engine heaved the human cattle into motion. With the doors shut it became very hot in the car. The small barred window near the roof did not let in sufficient air and soon there was a rising smell of perspiration. Janis' first thoughts proved right about the hole in the floor. This toilet arrangement caused intense embarrassment until some of the ladies made a makeshift curtain from a blanket.

Questions were asked, 'Where are we going?' Nobody knew. 'How long would they be away for?' Nobody told them and the guards said nothing. Numbed by the sudden change in his life Janis sat for a long period with his head between his knees and every so often his mother would stroke his head. Denial of the situation was impossible. The swaying of the car, the rhythmic beating of the wheels on the track, the impossibility of stretching out and the smell of the occupants forced the reality of the situation into Janis' consciousness. He was filled with apprehension and fear but little by little he told himself that he had to be strong. In the absence of his father he must now be the brave one and look after his mother. He looked over to her. Tears welling up in her eyes betrayed her sadness.

The train was shunted into a siding at Daugavpils, just inside the Latvian border. No one was allowed off but at least the freight door was opened for some cooling air. Janis looked around the car, 'What am I doing here, I am simply a teenager, what is my mother doing here and why are we with these people?' In the quiet of the siding people began to talk to each other, all equally bemused by the fact that their husbands had been described by the troika of officials as 'enemies of the people'.

People tried to figure out why they had been selected for this degrading experience. Many questions were asked, 'Is it because I speak Esperanto? Is it because I have a pen pal abroad? Is it because father was heard telling a joke about Stalin? Is it because I danced with the Japanese Ambassador at the Press Ball? Is it because my family has four cows and the rest of the villagers have only one?' People were looking for an explanation but nothing made sense.

The journey resumed and the train passed into Russia with a gentle rain falling. Janis thought that the drops that formed on the window and rolled down the bars were too much like tears for him to carry on looking at the scene. He turned his attentions to the hesitant conversations that took place. People wanted to talk but they only got so far before they wondered whether they had said too much. He soon realised what they all had in common. Their husbands and fathers had been participants in the Freedom Fight after the First World War or were members of the famous Latvian Riflemen during the war.

The conversations also included speculation as to what would happen to them at the destination and when they would be reunited with their men. It had become clear that Siberia was the destination but no one had a clear view as to what awaited them there. There was a great feeling of foreboding, especially as some talked about what they knew about the Soviet purge of the intelligentsia in Russia, but few facts were clear.

When the track curved, Janis could look along the length of the train. It seemed to go on forever. At the end of each alternate car was a machine gun post and men could be heard walking over the roof at times. Again he did not understand what he was experiencing. 'Everyone knows that war is imminent. Why was Stalin so interested in us? Surely there were bigger concerns?' These thoughts played through his mind. When the train stopped next to a similar one he could here Estonian voices and realised that what was happening was clearly not just limited to Latvia.

The train slowly made its way over the Russian countryside. It was the first time Janis had visited the country of his mother's birth and he was surprised how rundown and dirty the villages looked. Often straw roofs had collapsed and the boundaries of the house were marked by old bedsteads and other discarded metal objects. What he found surprising also was how few people there were. When he did see distant figures he thought at first they were scarecrows.

On one occasion, as Sonja looked further down the freight car Janis intently studied his mother's face. He noted her rather fine features and slender arms. Most Russian women seemed to be rather big and heavy but his mother was the exact opposite. She was wearing a delicately patterned summer dress. This was also quite different to that of the other women in the freight car who wore much sturdier garments. Somehow, Sonja must have felt the compassionate gaze of her son as she turned and gave a reassuring smile. Janis wondered if his mother had ever envisaged returning to her native country in a converted cattle car as a prisoner. 'How is she going to manage?' he queried. For as long as he had known, his mother had been used to a refined life that included afternoon teas and evening outings to the Opera House. He recalled that for his fifteenth birthday he had accompanied his parents and sister to the ballet, Cinderella. Further reminiscence was cut short as the brakes were screechingly applied and the train came to a stop in, what seemed to Janis, the middle of nowhere.

Janis could hear the guards running over the top of the train and others came along the side of the cars and banged them with hammers. *'Proverka* – checking,' the soldiers shouted as the freight car door was slid back. They pointed their bayonets for everyone to move to one end of the car. Then, one by one, the 'passengers' moved to the empty side as they were counted. This scene was repeated daily, sometimes twice daily and when there was a mistake in the counting the soldiers swore and lashed out at the nearest person. The list, it appeared, had to be correct. Janis understood that everyone had literally become a number. Being dead or alive was irrelevant. The person that stood behind that number with their unique history mattered even less.

After the checking, meagre rations were thrown in. Along with salty bread was dried and salted fish. The immediate effect was to bring on a terrible thirst. One cup of water was allocated per person. As the journey progressed the big decision for Janis and everyone became, 'Do I drink this in one go or sip it through the day?' For those that decided to sip the water there was not a moment's peace as they watched the cup until all the contents had gone lest someone knocked it over.

Once, and well into the journey, there was a heavy downpour and people put their cups as best they could through the barred window to catch the water as it dripped off the roof. The soldiers cried out that they would be shot, for such behaviour was forbidden. 'Why are they being so cruel?' Janis whispered to his mother. She shook her head ever so slightly as in disbelief and replied, 'They have their orders.'

On one occasion the train stopped in the middle of the night. Moonlight flooded in through the small barred window of the freight car. Janis thought about what might be happening to his sister who was older than him by two years and attended the ballet school in Riga. Noticing his mother was awake, he asked, 'Will Ginta be safe in the countryside?' Sonja did not immediately say anything. Instead she touched the small cross that hung around her neck. Her reply, 'With God's grace,' surprised Janis as he had not known his mother to be overly religious.

People suffered terribly from diarrhoea. Janis could hardly stand the smell in his carriage but he felt incredibly sorry for those affected. He was particularly concerned for the young baby that had been in the arms of his mother when they first entered the freight car. Cries had become shorter and his mother constantly stroked the child's brow.

Janis was already beginning to lose track of the days and so was not sure for how long they had been travelling when the baby died. It was marked by great wailing from his mother and crying from many of the others in the freight car. When the shouts of 'Proverka' came again the women took her baby to the guards. To the sound of sobbing that came from the mother's soul the baby was taken away. 'What are you going to do with him?' the mother's voice was hardly audible. The answer made her fall to her knees. Janis did not know enough Russian to understand what the guard had said and asked his mother to translate. Her face showed the shock she felt and she turned away without uttering anything. The sound of the soldier's reply imprinted on Janis' memory and it was some months later he understood that the soldier had responded to the mother's question with, 'We're gonna make him into soap.'

Article 58

March 8ᵗʰ 1953 – A Letter From Home

Janis' arm started to ache with Hilkka's head resting on it and he gradually eased it out from under the pillow whilst she slept on. He decided that he would not now try to catch up with his missed sleep. Instead, he got up, took a letter from his jacket pocket and went over to the bed by the window. Looking out he saw that people were still flooding into the centre of Moscow.

The letter was one of Janis' few personal possessions. It was from his mother in the Far North and had arrived as part of a batch that spanned almost three years of her life. He had wondered as to why the letters came in this way and an inefficient postal service could not have been the whole answer. Janis suspected that the NKVD officer that oversaw his mother had held onto them for some reason. Then he thought, 'Maybe, he wanted to go through them all in one go to make sure that he had not missed any secret code. Who knows? The main thing is that they got to me in the end.'

Janis had left the other letters in safe keeping with Ginta in Riga.

Carefully Janis opened the envelope and unfolded the letter written on very thin paper. He first admired his mother's stylish handwriting then read the letter to himself.

My dear son, my dear boy and Hilkka my beautiful daughter-in-law,

At last I received a letter from you. In fact, I received three and they all came in a small bundle neatly wrapped in string. When opening the first one, I reached a point where I could not keep my emotions still, tears were pouring out and it took quite a time to be able to read the letter properly.

I think I have always been strong in my spirit but there are weak moments too. How I long to see you both again!

From what you write it looks like my letters, of which I have sent quite a few, are not getting to you. But I will continue to write in the hope that they will one day and anyway, the process of setting pen to paper helps me to feel close to you.

It is so good to hear that you are enjoying a high cultural life in Riga. It sounds like it is an endless round of cinema, opera and ballet! I can imagine how wonderful it was to see Ginta in Cinderella. I remember so clearly when we all went to the Opera House to see the ballet. And for Ginta to play the Fairy Godmother, well all I can say is, I am very proud.

So, we are both in medicine! I am a nurse's assistant in Hospital Number 1 in Igarka and I really enjoy my work. I meet such a variety of people – some with impressive tattoos, which they are keen to show at every opportunity.

One recent patient was particularly interesting. He is a

geologist working on Project ▮. He remembers coming to Riga in 1940 as part of the summer celebrations. Do you remember those colourful marches along Brivibas Street?

The geologist remembers Riga as a beautiful city and talking with him brought back many happy memories.

Now, all the talk is of Project ▮. Of course, no one knows what this project is about but it means that Igarka is no longer a quiet place. It is a real city.

The theatre here in Igarka is on the same level as the best theatres in Moscow and Leningrad. Most of the actors came from Leningrad and Moscow and the hospital is full of excellent doctors. Admittedly some of them are working as orderlies!

We have two professional dancers, Mr. and Mrs. Suvorin from Leningrad and they have established a ballet school. What is truly amazing is that I went to the Suvorin's class when I was a young girl. Of course they are quite old now but their passion for ballet is still the same. Despite the vastness of Siberia it is, sometimes, a small world.

Professor Cibulnik from Moscow Music Academy has organised a string ensemble and a former opera singer, Vasiljev, has established a choir. I went along to the auditions for the choir and Vasiljev said that I have a very good voice. We practise whenever we can. We sing mainly Russian songs but I am keen to teach the choir some Latvian folksongs. Do you still play the harmonica? Whenever I hear one I think of our evenings in the Far North.

Article 58

We have a cinema and there is sometimes dancing during the intermissions. Old dances from tsarist times are the most popular. When people try the new Tango and Foxtrot it is stopped by the authorities. And so it should be. Such close proximity. Really!

Mirdza Kangare has established a school for sculptors and I know that many Latvians are attending her art classes.

This summer has been unusually hot. For several weeks it has been over plus 30 degrees. But we have been busy in the hospital because for some reason people have been getting sick. Maybe gasses have been released from the permafrost?

If I could have control of one project, I would build a railway over the tundra, taiga, permafrost and swamps from Moscow to Igarka and beyond. Do you remember the Far North with its clouds of moskas in the summer and dense icy fog in the winter? Our great engineers must be able to tame such a wild place and think how marvellous it would be to get to Moscow in under ten days.

Here are all kinds of people. Those of us under Article 58 live much like everyone else. The only difference is that twice a month we must register with the local commander.

Hilkka, I hope that you are finding life interesting in Riga. I know that you must miss your family and I often talk about you with Pauli and the girls. Girls, what am I saying! They are beautiful young women just like yourself. Your father lives in a block that is not too far away. Last week we met, by chance, at the cinema on our day off. Battleship Potemkin was showing. Just looking at the Director, Eisenstein's name takes me back to Alberts Street. Janis, have you told Hilkka that the Director's father designed our beautiful house?

I had a dream last night in which you both came through the gate at our old summerhouse. You were both well and happy but the strange thing was you were wearing birch bark shoes of the sort we used to have in the Far North. Maybe it means my thoughts are with you in every step you take.

One short story before I finish. A man in our block died suddenly about a year ago leaving behind a dog. My heart went out to this poor creature, the dog of course! The man was known to be a drinker and had a foul temper. The dog, it turns out, had been constantly thrashed and left to starve and yet was loyal to its owner. This emaciated and beaten dog was found sitting by the owner, who had died in the night. The long-suffering animal was taken in by a kind neighbour. At first it was scared and would hide or quiver if there was a quick movement or an unexpected noise. Yet, it quickly responded to strokes and proper food. It is such a loving dog and I often pat its head when I see it out with its new owner. It makes you think doesn't it?

I will finish now. My prayers are with you both.

Yours lovingly

Mamma

Ps. The geologist's only regret is that he wasn't able to keep the suit.

Janis enjoyed reading his mother's letters. She was so ironic and subtle that any criticism of the Soviet system would have passed without detection by the NKVD censor. However, the censor had crossed out the number of the project and Janis could not help being amused with his diligence when everyone, it seemed, in the Soviet Union had heard of Project 503.

The letters were bittersweet for Janis. He found it interesting to hear about his mother's life but, just as in his letters to her, he knew that his mother was not telling him about the harsh side of life in the Far North. There were only hints that life was not as rosy as her letter portrayed. One hint that Janis noticed related to the tattoos of the patients. He knew that there was a prison camp just outside the city and that criminals were well known for having elaborate tattoos. Janis recalled a time when he had come face to face with criminals and involuntarily formed a tight fist. He pondered on his mother's job and thought, 'Nursing these filthy men, full of lice and with a dreadful attitude to women must be hell.'

Janis thought about Hilkka and their room that they had just given up in Riga with a drunkard for a landlord and a prostitute for a neighbour. He wondered whom his mother was living next to. Sonja did not write about where she lived and as such Janis could not help feeling that it was probably indescribable. 'Anyway,' he thought, 'the good news is that Mamma is out of the taiga and away from Plague Lakes.'

Prompted by Sonja's letter, Janis recalled going to see a big march on Brivibas Street, which took place soon after the Soviet occupation. He had not seen the like of such in Riga and stood in amazement at the people who shouted communist slogans and waved red flags. He was surprised that he did not recognise a single face and the people seemed to be overly dressed. It was a warm summer's day yet the men were in thick suits and some women wore coats. Many Russian buses parked at the bus station aroused his suspicion that the demonstrators had been shipped in to show support for the Soviet administration.

It was clear to Janis that his mother was telling him in the letter that many Russians, including the geologist that she had met, had been imported for the marches to celebrate the arrival of the Soviet administration. Janis was always surprised at the elaborate conceit that Russia undertook to show the rest of the world what good neighbours they were.

Sonja's ironic hand showed through with the reference to Project 503. Janis thought, 'Despite the secret police, censorship and control of the press, it is common knowledge that vast numbers of workers are required on a building project - and probably a railway.'

Janis knew that his mother considered the Far North to be untamable. His thoughts went back to the day of his accident and having to slowly travel over swamps and tundra. He said to himself, 'If Project 503 sets out to conquer the taiga and tundra, it is doomed to failure. How many lives will be lost before the Far North proves to be the victor?'

The story of the dog did make Janis think. He was sure that his mother had added this simple story as a parable. Despite meeting some truly nasty characters he had found Russians to be generally kind and loyal, but clearly they were being treated harshly and cruelly. Janis wondered whether his mother was writing this story of the dog to give hope that their beating would stop one day and that humanity towards others would return.

Janis was looking forward to seeing his mother but he wondered whether she would be in good health. He feared that the biting cold that settles into the bone marrow must have taken its toll. He pondered, 'Mamma does not write about any illness but is that because she never complains?'

Janis began to think about his mother's life and about how much of it was hidden from him. He mused, 'Until this letter, I didn't even know that Mamma went to ballet classes. What else don't I know about her? Probably quite a lot. But what I do know is that she was always there, always positive and always thinking about what we needed to do to survive. I was a teenager when I left for Siberia and wouldn't have lasted even through the first summer without her.'

Janis' thoughts turned to his years in Siberia.

Midsummer 1941

On midsummer's eve, singing started in one freight car and spread along the train. This was the night when Latvians traditionally headed to the countryside to celebrate the summer solstice in song and dance. In the middle of *Tumša Nakte, Zaļa Zāle,* Dark Night, Green Grass, shouts from the guards could be heard above the massed voices, 'Quiet or we shoot.' The singing rose in defiance and Janis thought, 'Surely they could not shoot everyone?' Then shots rang out. The singing suddenly stopped.

The train was deep into Russia on its slow journey east when news of the war reached Janis and the other deportees. A civilian train had pulled up close and news filtered along that the might of the Soviet army was pitched against the German forces. There was talk that Stalin had addressed the nation and called for the entire Soviet people to rise against the fascists and defend the motherland. People on the other train looked suspiciously at those on Janis', which was clearly full of Nazi sympathisers.

The news of war gave rise in Janis to hope of a swift return to Latvia. He thought that if the Germans could quickly overcome the Soviet forces then they could return home. He knew that he could not voice such ideas, as clearly this would prove that he actually was an enemy of the people. These thoughts were not without a sense of guilt as he had learnt at school that the Germans were the old enemy. The barons had suppressed the Latvian peasants for centuries. Nevertheless, inwardly, Janis hoped for a quick German victory.

The pace of the train slowed further as it had to let pass other trains that were full of soldiers, tanks and guns. Inexorably though it made its way east and crossed the Ural Mountains then the River Oba. They passed through a station called Taiga and then it pulled into a station called Achinska. After some considerable delay the train turned south and at Adalima it stopped and everyone was ordered off.

For several days the large group of increasingly dejected deportees sat in the big square behind the station at Adalima. Each day more trains arrived and Janis ran to see if any contained his father, but they only spilled out more tired and sick women and children. Some family members were reunited but not with their husbands and fathers. Janis was one of the oldest boys and he helped to make a bonfire on which leftover scraps of stale bread were toasted. In the now overcrowded square everyone slept on their bundles. Janis kept close to his mother. The days were warm but the nights were cool and he did what he could to ensure that his mother was sufficiently warm.

After a few days a large number of horse drawn carts arrived. Men in uniforms and civilian clothes walked through the crowd. They argued amongst themselves as they picked out people from the mass. These were the administrators from the collective farms that had come to select their labour. One of the ladies near Janis muttered, 'Only by looking at our teeth could they make us feel more like slaves.' Although Janis was one of the older boys he was small for his age and did not stand out. Neither he nor his mother was picked straight away.

Later, more carts arrived and Janis and his mother's belongings were loaded on. Eventually the caravan set off. Thin horses pulled the carts and bored looking NKVD officers escorted them. Janis, his mother and the rest of the contingent walked wearily in their wake. The trip lasted several days and at night they simply slept under the carts.

Janis' only amusement was watching the most senior of the NKVD officers, who was the only one permitted to ride on the carts, being bounced about. The suspension on the old carts was almost non-existent and the officer was continually bumped and jolted over the countless ruts that crisscrossed each other. He began to resemble a rag doll with his head constantly flopping from one side to another.

Janis was surprised that there were no roads. It was only later when the autumn rains started that he understood the reason for this. It was easier to drive on untouched ground. Where it was black and sticky the cartwheels sank in. He even learnt that there was a Russian word, *rasputitsa* that was used for the period of rain and mud that made Russian roads impassable before the winter freeze.

The trip ended at Kulichki in Beryozovska county, Krasnoyarsk region. The village appeared suddenly. One minute the carts were heading up an incline and the next moment they were in the main village street.

Janis had already got used to how poor looking the villages were in Russia but the wooden houses in this one appeared particularly run down. The gates to these dwellings, which were richly carved, intrigued Janis. They held such promise but they only led onto squalor.

Janis, his mother and two other families were set down in front of a sad looking, abandoned wooden house. The windowpanes were stuffed with rags. Janis and his mother made their way into the house. The other families followed them and each looked at the others in bewilderment when they found that it consisted of one large room with very sparse furnishing and no beds. Later that day, long grass was cut and Sonja laid it in the room so that at least they had rudimentary bedding.

Janis had always had his own bedroom. Now he slept in the same space as six other people. At first he was self-conscious and would try to get dressed under the covers of his bedding. Seeing other people in states of undress was initially disconcerting but gradually his sensitivities changed. Also, the ladies erected some curtains to protect their modesty and then as it grew colder everyone went to sleep fully clothed.

So, daily life in Siberia began for Janis and the others.

Mid-Siberia was not without interest for the boys who had arrived with the caravan. Janis, as the oldest, quickly became the leader and they set about exploring the territory. Janis' house was located at the side of a large square. Some of the houses around this were built up on stacks to about a metre. Janis later learnt that this kept the entrances above the snow in winter. As the newly arrived boys walked around the square the locals watched them intently. All kept their distance. When the boys approached, the onlookers disappeared.

Janis soon learned that virtually all the village men had been conscripted into the Red Army. Only young boys and old or handicapped males remained. The rest of the villagers were girls and women.

After a few days when it was clear to the locals that the newly arrived boys were not going anywhere quickly the village boys started to approach. Contact was restricted initially to jeering and the occasional clod of mud being hurled.

The three foremen of the collective farm were all lame. Nevertheless, each morning they rode on horseback through the village and with their whips they knocked on doors and windows calling people to work in the fields. Janis and the newly arrived inhabitants quickly assembled but the local women were busy from early hours lighting big Russian stoves in their kitchens and preparing meals for when they returned, so it was late into the morning when the working party set off to the meadows. It was still quite a walk to where they worked and by the time that duties actually commenced, it was nearly noon. After a few hours there was a stop for lunch. Sometimes this consisted of soup or boiled potatoes but mainly it was a barrel of water accompanied by salty tasting bread. Occasionally, it was the 'Kiril ovskaya lunch', which was just a bowl of water. At first, Janis was surprised to see the Russian women sitting together during their break exactly like monkeys do picking through their fur. They were looking for lice and soon all of the new recruits joined in this social habit.

No one was eager to work it seemed, especially the new arrivals. They waited for news of their men folk and developments on the battlefront.

Gradually, Janis began to enjoy his duties. He had to either scythe the grass or transport hay with a horse cart. He had never ridden a horse before or driven a cart. The small woolly Siberian horses were difficult to control but he enjoyed being out in the open air and with the warm sun he soon developed a healthy-looking complexion.

In their spare time the small group of boys, which Janis had become the leader of, organised the occasional raid on vegetable patches and 'inspected' village cellars that were built separately from the houses. These contained *krinkas*, jugs filled with creamy milk. Siberian cows produced little but the milk was lovely and thick. A small amount was regularly pilfered, which did not go down well with the women in the village. They were already rather suspicious of the boys. Janis understood that this was because the newly arrived inhabitants had been described as fascists. With husbands away fighting against the Germans it was surprising to him that the villagers were not more hostile.

Relationships with the local boys remained distant and cool for a while. This was largely because they did not speak the same language. Only one of the boys, Ivars, spoke Russian and somehow he managed to bridge the divide.

Ivars was tall for his age and was slightly uncoordinated. In the quiet times that there were, and whilst sitting in the village square, the two boys told each other a little of their backgrounds. Ivars was also from Riga and lived in a suburb called Aganskalns. He too had been deported on June 14th. Ivars had seen for himself the army trucks gathering at Uzvaras Laukums, Victory Square the day before but had not told his parents about this. Ivars often berated himself for this omission as they could have immediately started to pack and run off before the troika of officials arrived preventing any escape.

Ivars spoke Russian because his mother was Russian and she continued to use her native language in their house. Janis wondered how come his own mother spoke perfect Latvian and never used Russian at home whilst Ivars' mother spoke Latvian with a heavy Russian accent.

Little by little the two groups of youths mingled. The Russian boys were occasionally open-mouthed when they were told about life in Latvia. They were especially intrigued by the idea of having toilets inside the house. 'Do you shit in the living room?' one boy asked.

Life in the mid-Siberian village slowly moved on. Summer was passing and the gang of boys roamed further afield. They found that in some of the surrounding villages there were potatoes, flour and eggs but no one was prepared to sell them. Money was useless as there was virtually nothing to buy – not even soap. Instead of soap the villagers used the alkaline liquid that was obtained after soaking ashes in water. It did little to prevent body odour. For a while Janis was not keen to get too close to the locals but this was mainly because they persistently chewed something that made their breath reek. It turned out that this was called Cheremska, which was a wild form of garlic. It was full of vitamins and was the best prevention of scurvy. The women gathered it all summer and preserved it in salt for use in the winter. Hesitantly at first, Janis and the new arrivals started to chew Cheremska and over time they noticed that the locals' breath did not smell as bad!

After a while Janis and the other deportees wondered why food seemed to be in such short supply. The summer was short but it seemed that the soil was so rich and fertile that even if you left potato peel on the ground it would root.

The villagers did not want money but were prepared to barter for their produce. Under the direction of his mother, Janis used some of the clothes that the Russian Army officer had thrown into the truck to obtain provisions and the best deal he struck was with one of the foremen at the Collective Farm. The foreman was taken with Janis' father's Latvian Rifleman's uniform, from which the badges had been removed. Whenever Janis saw the old lame man in his father's uniform he felt sick. Wearing the uniform the foreman shouted more loudly and used his whip more often. Janis pondered on the effect that a uniform had on the average Russian.

Janis was sure that it must have been painful for his

mother to trade the uniform but he had a feeling that the stock of potatoes that he got for it would be vital later on. Little did he appreciate that Sonja's thought to make the transaction would stop them starving in their first mid-Siberian winter.

Around the harvest time there many new arrivals in the village. It was clear that the Germans had advanced far into Russia and the new arrivals were evacuees that included many families of high-ranking army officers. The officers' wives treated everyone, locals and deportees alike, with utter disdain.

Article 58

Mid-Siberian Winter 1941

When the sunny days and summer blooms were over the rain came in heavier and heavier downpours. The earth turned black like it had been charred. The migrating birds had to rest in the deluges and they walked over the fields with their heads bowed mimicking the poor inhabitants of the settlement who were forced out in all weathers.

After the rains, winter slammed its icy boot onto the ground. When it started to snow it did not stop until it was up to about a metre. Then a bone-chilling cold set in. The summer had not been easy but none of the new inhabitants were prepared for the hardships of winter. The talk was all about survival.

Janis had hoped that with the onset of the season they would be returning home courtesy of a German rout of the Soviets but this had not happened. However, the omens remained good. News filtered to them that the Germans had reached Moscow. 'Surely,' thought Janis, 'it won't be long now before the Red Army completely collapses.'

In the gloom of the hut one evening Janis and his mother were together and he asked, 'If the German army has advanced so far do you think that they've driven the Russians out of Latvia?' Sonja whipped her head around to check that no one was nearby and then quietly replied, 'Please Jani, you must keep any such thoughts to yourself.' Janis suddenly felt that he had put his mother's life in danger by just verbalising his thoughts but the possibility of a German victory seemed to be close. Janis often went to sleep thinking about his return to Riga and being reunited with his father. He was also conscious that the more he had these thoughts the more he became an enemy of the people.

Janis' family had not been particularly religious and Janis was only an infrequent visitor to church. Now, he prayed each night for a quick German victory. As the weather turned colder he feared for his mother's health. Despite enduring the physical work in the meadows she looked far too fragile to last through a prolonged winter. Even then, Janis did not appreciate just how long and severe the winter would be.

Janis' main winter duty was to prepare the kindling wood for the collective farm. He set out each day with a group of teenagers and some women from the collective farm and together they waded through the snow carrying axes and saws. Janis was the only one with a pair of skis and he often shared their use with Ivars. When they arrived at the edge of the forest they cut down anything that they could and in this way they found that they had to travel a little further each day for their wood. The logs for the collective farm were stacked neatly for later collection by horse-pulled sleigh. At the end of the day the boys brought back their own logs which they managed to do by balancing them on two separate hand-pulled sleighs and guiding them home.

There was always plenty of wood for the fire but it was green and did not burn well. This combined with an inefficient stove meant that the large room was rarely warm. Anyone who had worked outside took a long time to warm up and dry out. Occasionally, and always under the cover of a blizzard, the teenagers would raid the abandoned houses and take whatever was wooden. Tables, benches, fences and in fact anything that could be burnt made its way back to their room to be fed into the large stove. Then, for a brief period, the large room became quite warm. To the inhabitants there were odd periods of cosiness but 'cosy' could not describe the shabby condition, the threadbare clothes and windows full of rags to stop the chill wind from blowing through.

The clothes were not suitable for a Siberian winter. Only a few of the deportees in the village had fur hats or thick coats. Many of them had not taken any winter wear as they had been told that they were only being moved temporarily. Sonja had asked the village blacksmith to make needles from old nails and under her guidance the ladies started to make winter clothing from whatever they had. Quilted jackets were made out of blankets and long-johns were made from sheets. Nothing was wasted. The wool in old and worn out clothes was salvaged and made into patchwork hats and gloves. It was long and hard work in the gloom of the hut. Only the shoes were supplied for them. These were very primitive and were constructed from tree bark. Whilst primitive, Janis was grateful that the shoes kept out the increasing chill.

Janis was ordered, occasionally, to work in the oil press. This was his favourite job because it was warm inside the tiny factory that made oil from rapeseeds and hemp. Inside there were many different cogs, pulleys and a big roasting kettle. A sad looking horse walking in a continual circle powered the press and an old man in an oily jacket and floppy hat supervised the whole operation. A small lamp and the fire under the kettle produced a flickering light and with the workers' impoverished clothing it was a scene straight from a medieval painting.

On a Sunday when the workload was less, Janis' house was the meeting place for his country folk. Stories were told and songs were sung. In fact, a song or two was sung every evening. Janis had managed to keep hold of his harmonica and he had become an accomplished player. A few favourites were repeated but they never seemed to run out of new songs.

By the light of a small lamp Sonja made pretty embroidered items out of scraps of cloth. Embroidery had been her hobby and she was now able to make a few kopeks from selling them. Of course, the locals did not need such things. She sold them to the officers' wives.

Janis was fascinated by the lives of the villagers. They slept in the same clothes as they worked in and used a rolled up jacket as a pillow. He paid particular attention to their management of livestock. In the winter the locals kept their cattle in enclosures that were made of wicker fence panels that lessened the penetrating wind but it was just as cold inside as out. The hardy cows survived the harshest weather because they had thick coats but if they gave birth, the owner had to be there or the newborn would soon die. The calf would be brought inside the house and tied to a post. When it lifted its tail it was time to place a pan there and if this was missed the floor was covered in cow pee. Under the kitchen table there invariably was a pen with chickens and possibly a lamb or piglet.

As the winter went on Janis was proud that his mother was coping remarkably well. However, his thought was that if it came to having to tie a calf up inside the house or having chickens under the kitchen table this would be too much for her. One evening whilst everyone settled close the stove, he asked his mother, 'Can you imagine living with your animals?' He was surprised when she replied, 'Man is a creature that can get used to anything, and I think that this is the best definition of him.' Janis was wondering just what he would be capable of doing to survive when another lady joined in and added, 'Did you know that your mother quoted Dostoevsky's 'House of the Dead'. Well, we are in good company, Dostoevsky was sent to Siberia for four years hard labour.'

The winter was bitterly cold. There were no thermometers but Janis could tell that it was colder than anything that he had experienced before. On the coldest days he could hear a faint jangling sound as he breathed out. His breath immediately turned to ice crystals. It was on the first day of extreme cold that Janis realised the dangers associated with the sub-zero temperatures. After being outside for a short while and wearing a hat and scarf made of old blankets, he came into the house and quickly took off the scarf that was protecting him from the biting wind and unforgiving cold. In doing so, he ripped off a large piece of skin around his mouth where the material had frozen to his face. The damaged area turned black at first but later recovered.

After this experience, Sonja reminded Janis to cover his face with a cream that she made, which contained mostly pig fat.

As the winter wore on there was bad news for the enemies of the people. News filtered to the village of the glorious victories of the Soviet Army. The German Army, just like that of Napoleon, had been forced to retreat. Janis felt crushed. All hopes of a quick return to Latvia were dashed. Janis and his house of Latvians were not the only ones to feel despair. News continually reached them of yet another officer's wife in the village being left a widow.

There were many discussions that winter about how such a state of affairs could have been reached. For Janis it had all come as a shock. His life had been comfortable and settled. He had heard of political turmoil in Europe but his focus had been on his schoolwork and as a diligent pupil he was doing well. He remembered the reports about the Spanish Civil War and of Germany Invading Poland but it all seemed so remote. What was more real to him was the sense of Riga being a vibrant city full of activity and trade. When he heard his President address the nation and say, 'You remain in your place, I shall remain in mine,' Janis was reassured. Soon after the address the Russians entered Riga. Everything changed on that day.

Article 58

Latvian Riflemen

In the depths of winter, with the long nights and constant sub-zero temperatures, there was time after the duties of the day had been completed to sit in the hut and contemplate or participate in far-ranging discussions. A constant question that Janis tried to answer was why his father had been classified as an enemy of the people. It made no sense to him. His father had served his country in the Latvian Riflemen and had a respected position in society. One evening, whilst sitting next to his mother in the flickering light of two candles and a smoky oil lamp, Janis asked her to tell him more about his father's history.

Sonja said, 'Jani, it is time that you knew more about your father's past, but don't get worried, there are only good things to hear. Your father didn't want to talk about his experiences and would like to have forgotten much of it.' Sonya settled back and Janis realised that he was about to be given a family history that he had not heard before.

Sonja continued, 'Pappa was a brilliant student. Of course he didn't tell me this himself but Grandpappa showed me his certificates and his school reports. After graduating from school Pappa studied chemistry under Wilhelm Ostwald at Riga Polytechnicum. I'm sure that you have heard of our famous Nobel Prize winner. Pappa had a great career ahead of him and could have gone on to study in St. Petersburg or

Moscow. Then, it seemed out of nowhere, the First World War began. Pappa was not only a brilliant scholar, he was also a patriot. With the Germans advancing towards Latvia, he was one of the first to join the Latvian Riflemen. Pappa wanted to keep out the old enemy.' 'Ah yes, the German Barons,' Janis added.

Sonja took a sip of her pine needle tea and continued, 'Can you imagine how proud your father was to have served in the Tsar's newly formed battalions? They were the first Latvian forces commanded by Latvians. Grandpappa once told me how there was a great celebration in Riga as volunteers returned from factories deep in Russia to be part of the battalions. After training, Pappa was made a Lieutenant in the Riga Latvian Riflemen Regiment and led his men to battle.' Janis remembered the picture of his father that stood on a table in their apartment in Riga. In this, his father was seen saluting in his Rifleman's uniform. He then remembered the foreman of the collective farm wearing the same uniform and felt an anger emerging.

Sonja continued, 'Oh what a terrible time they endured. The two forces, Russians, supported by battalions of Latvian Riflemen, faced the Germans and each was dug into their own trenches. Then, in the deepest part of the winter of 1916 and 1917 the Russian generals decided to mount a surprise attack. Except, the Germans were prepared. Pappa told that he had to lead his men out of the trenches and into the gunfire that opened up from the German positions. It was carnage. Men fell and the wounded simply froze on the battlefield. Somehow, your father and some of his men managed to break the German defence but it was wasted effort. One hundred and fifty metres of frozen land was captured with the loss of over thirty thousand men. Pappa talked about it only once with me and never raised the subject again.

'Jani, what I am going to tell you now is not what your father has ever told me in detail. These are my thoughts and understanding of what these soldiers faced in the spring of 1917.... The armies were well dug in and there was no great breakthrough on either side. Between the fighting there were long periods of waiting for orders. During this, the Latvian Riflemen had time to think about what happened to them on the battlefield and what was happening further afield in Russia. They would have had the same discussions as almost everyone else in the Russian empire. The Bolsheviks' voice was strong and reached the men in the trenches. Lenin was against the war and that appealed to many who had seen the wasteful bloodshed and the arrogant approach of the Tsar's generals.

'Soon after these futile Christmas battles, the forces heard that the Tsar had abdicated. Maybe it is hard to imagine but try to put yourself in these soldiers' position. They went to war fighting for Tsar Nicholas II against the Germans. The threat of the Germans remained but, with the Tsar deposed, many of the Latvian Riflemen wondered for whom they were fighting. Many began to believe that there could be a better future, as promised by the Bolsheviks. This would be a future that did not involve sending young men into battle ill-equipped to face a hail of bullets.'

After taking another sip of tea, Sonja continued, 'In May 1917, after sitting in the trenches for months, first tired and cold, then hungry, many Riflemen grew angry. What is more they had a choice to make. Were they with the Bolsheviks or against them? This was the choice faced by all. Most of the Latvian Regiments transferred their loyalty to the Bolsheviks. They became known as *Latviešu Sarkanie Strēlnieki*, Red Latvian Riflemen. There were others that opposed the Bolsheviks and they sided with the White Guard in the Civil War.'

Janis sat for a while taking in the scene of the battlefield and the men in the trenches trying to decide which side of destiny they should be on. Eventually he asked, 'Why did Pappa not talk about the war?' Sonja explained, 'Some experiences are too dreadful to put into words. If you've had comrades killed outright by a bullet or frozen to death as wounded soldiers; or you've shot an enemy, this is not the sort of thing that is easy to talk of. I think that also Pappa didn't want to talk about his past because he was not proud to have helped usher in communism. He once said that he had seen how the Bolsheviks treated their own people and could see no good coming from a future under their control.'

Janis again sat for a while, taking in this new information. Eventually he asked, 'Please can you carry on. How did you meet with Pappa?'

Sonja, continued, 'Your father came to St. Petersburg with the Red Latvian Riflemen in November 1917 and saved my life.

'My father, may the sand rest lightly on him, was a merchant. We were not old aristocracy but Father was wealthy and powerful; just the target for the Bolsheviks' anger. After the Tsar abdicated, all my neighbours and family friends feared for their lives, but with the Provisional Government under George Lvov and then later Alexander Kerensky there was some stability. That lasted until October when the Bolsheviks seized power. Then, St. Petersburg was in turmoil. It was a great opportunity for everyone to seek revenge on anyone who had more than they did. Mobs rampaged. I hid for months in the attic of our house but one evening I had to quickly escape as the house was set on fire. In the street outside there was a mob intent on trouble. I was grabbed by a soldier and bundled into a truck. I had no idea of what my fate was going to be. Then another soldier came to the back of the truck. He looked at me and shouted, 'Let this one out.' I was afraid because everyone knew how the soldiers raped even young girls. This soldier was your father. When I was released from the truck he asked me, 'Where can you go that is safe?' He sounded so kind and genuine, I immediately trusted him with my life.

'When the fighting in St. Petersburg had died down, Pappa was sent, as part of the Red Army, to other fronts of the Russian Civil War.

'In 1920, and after Latvia became independent, many thousands of Red Latvian Riflemen returned to Latvia. Reinis returned with them but on his way, he visited St. Petersburg, searched for me and proposed marriage.'

Janis sat in the gloom of the hut thinking of his parents leaving Russia together. After a while he asked, 'Pappa didn't fight for independence then?'

'No, independence had been achieved whilst Pappa was in Russia. I once asked your father whether he had ever thought that Latvia would be independent. He said that until he had experienced the anarchy of the civil war he had never honestly considered it possible that Russia would give away its Baltic territory. He said that the strength of the western powers and the disarray in Russia provided an opportunity to create an independent Latvia, but he was worried that when the dust settled the bear would be keen to get back its old hunting ground.'

Janis was delighted to have heard about his parents' past but he still felt confused and voiced this to his mother, 'Pappa was a hero. He helped the Bolsheviks take control of Russia. Why are they punishing him now?' Sonya replied, 'This, I cannot answer. All I know is that the loyalty of senior army officers was rewarded with arrests for being traitors or saboteurs. The mind of a man who can push his boot onto the neck of all those that supported him cannot be fathomed.' Although Janis was sitting next to his mother and near the stove, he suddenly felt a chill run down his spine. He understood that Stalin's shadow was long and dark.

Spring 1942

Somehow the winter softened its icy grip. Then there was a standoff between the retreating winter and approaching spring. There were no signs of growth but the tapping of newly rising sap in the birch trees foretold the coming of warmer days. Janis enjoyed collecting the clear flowing sap. Every mouthful of the liquid seemed to say to him that he had survived and he too could now reawaken.

In the spring Janis turned sixteen and became a fully-fledged deportee. He was given papers that described him as 'a child of an enemy of the people' and he had to have these signed once a month by a man who arrived from the Regional Office. The officialdom surprised Janis. The collective farm could not organise a rota system, yet lists of its citizens especially deportees were kept with meticulous efficiency.

Although record-keeping had been developed into a high art, the overall system appeared to Janis to be a mixture of chance, bureaucracy and cruelty. Just as with his sister, some of the deportees' children had been left behind in the rush to exile people. One of the ladies in the village was reunited with her daughter who had been given permission in Riga to visit her mother. Janis heard that many tears were shed at the reunion and even more shed when the child was reclassified as a deportee and barred from returning.

Janis longed to see his sister but hoped that she would not suddenly arrive.

New arrivals that spring included two older teenagers than Janis. They were given some instruction on how to drive a tractor and then were ordered to plough the field. Janis became their assistant. He had to sit on the back of the tractor and lift the ploughshare at each turn. When they had to plough into the night to finish their allocated work Janis walked in front of the tractor with a lamp.

On one occasion the old tractor broke down. The boys looked at it and kicked the wheels but had no idea how to fix it. The older boys got out their cigarettes that were allocated to tractor drivers and smoked these while they thought about what they could do. Janis was always amused by the name of the tobacco, *Smertj Gitleru* – Death to Hitler. They agreed that smoking the tobacco would be their only voluntary war effort but Janis was not sure how it would help in Hitler's demise.

The name of the tobacco might have amused the boys but the tractor's breakdown proved to be highly stressful for the youngsters. The foreman threatened them with imprisonment for sabotage. Eventually they managed to coax the tractor back to life and later found that such threats were customary under the Soviet system. The operators were always blamed. Fear, it seemed, was the preferred tool of control rather than training and education.

Traditionally tractor drivers had a separate existence from the rest of the village. They slept near their workplace in a trailer. Here they lived alongside women. Now, men were in short supply and only the foreman remained who had a paralysed arm. Nevertheless, he managed to do the work of three men and slept with a different woman each night. Janis and his workmates were billeted in a small hut nearby. The noises emanating from the trailer at night were disturbing and for a teenage boy highly erotic. The noises must have aroused the other young men too, as one night they decided to try to peer through the windows of the foreman's trailer.

Quietly the youngsters made their way to the trailer. One of them stood on a box and looked in. Suddenly the box gave way and the boy stumbled back with a muffled 'ouch'. There was cursing from inside the caravan and all the boys raced back to their hut. Later, when it was clear that the foreman was not coming their way, the one that peered in was asked about what he saw. The only thing he said was, 'The foreman has got a dreadfully hairy arse.'

At the end of May, Janis and his mother, together with five other families, were ordered to pack. They were told that they were going further north for the summer to fish. They packed all they had but decided to leave the unwieldy skis as summer was fast approaching.

Janis' friend, Ivars and his mother were not amongst those ordered to go north. Rather formally the boys shook hands and said that they would see each other at the end of the summer. Then they were off. The small woolly Siberian horses pulled carts with their wheels half submerged in the liquid spring mud and the contingent walked behind through the seemingly endless taiga. The sun's rays shone through the trees above but the paths were murky and dank. All around there were fallen trees and branches covered with a shaggy grey moss. It was a forest that seemed to Janis to be without end. It was largely made up of larch with the occasional huge cedar or spruce and even more rarely a silver birch or aspen. Whilst it seemed interesting at first to be travelling through the taiga it became depressingly monotonous.

The trip on the carts lasted several days and on the way they met up with other carts heading in the same direction. They crossed the Uzhur Mountains that were covered in tulips, irises and lilies. Then at a train station they were ordered back onto the same sort of freight cars that had taken them east the year before. Janis suddenly realised that they would not be returning after summer and felt a fool that he had been tricked into leaving his skis.

After another long, slow and painfully cramped journey, the miserable looking cargo was put off the train at the bank of the River Yenisei near to Krasnoyarsk. Janis had never seen such a wide river before and he was told that it was the largest river that flowed into the Arctic Ocean. The shore was full of people and he heard many foreign languages including what he took to be English.

Janis and Sonja were put together with a group of Latvians and Volga Germans who had been waiting a number of days on the riverbank. Janis learned that there had been an autonomous German republic near to the Volga in the Soviet Union. That evening, he talked about their arrival with Sonja and some other Latvians. There was general amusement at the convoluted reasoning of the Soviet authorities. The Volga Germans had explained that Russian military intelligence suspected that thousands of saboteurs and spies were in the area. As none had been found it was clear to the authorities that the Volga Germans must be hiding them. The Volga Germans were charged with 'concealing enemies' and the republic was liquidated. All the inhabitants were moved east. Sonja concluded, 'Janis, at least you will understand Russian logic at the end of this adventure.'

Overnight, all the deportees stayed in wooden barracks. Never before had Janis seen so many bed bugs. Sleep was short and restless. Every time he woke he thought he heard the sound of bed bugs marching and ordering commands.

After a few days a flotilla arrived to take the awaiting deportees further north. The flotilla consisted of ten vessels including barges and lighters. A big steamship, the Vyacheslav Molotov, towed the whole convoy. The Latvians were put on the steamship along with Volga Germans, Moldavians wearing white linen pants and embroidered shirts and Kalmyks. This was the first time that Janis had met a Kalmyk and was interested to learn that they were Buddhist Mongols living in Russia near the western shore of the Caspian Sea. The autonomous Republic of Kalmykia had been liquidated and many Kalmyks were deported.

As the trip progressed the river widened, and passing the River Angara its clear blue water cut like a blade into the yellowish waters of the Yenisei.

The river grew wider and wider. At one point it was so wide that Janis struggled to make out the other bank. One afternoon a storm blew up and waves quickly whipped up which tossed the barges around. Cold rain soaked the heavy hearts of all on board and many below decks were seasick.

The journey was punctuated with moments of humour – at least for the boys onboard. The toilet on the ship was simply an overhang at the back of the boat. Once, the rail snapped and an unfortunate soldier squatting there toppled back into the cold river. The boys heard the yell of the man as he fell backward with his trousers around his ankles. 'Man overboard,' they shouted with glee and the miserable looking soldier was unceremoniously hauled back on board to barely suppressed laughter from the boys.

The further north the ship steamed the less populated the bank of the river became. Janis had not realised just how vast Russia was. Somewhere along the route they crossed the Arctic Circle. Occasionally the flotilla would halt and put some people out. Janis and his mother were among the last to leave the boat when the ship reached its final destination.

On midsummer's day, June 1942, the flotilla reached Igarka and there the group was divided up. Janis and his mother were put into a smaller cutter along with ten or so Latvians, a few Volga Germans and the Moldavians. They travelled north through the white night. The sun never set. Occasionally it would dip behind the treetops on the far shore and then reappear as a red ball. Janis found it difficult to sleep and in the early morning he saw how calm the river was except for the fanning wake of the cutter. Ahead it was like a mirror which reflected the distant hills, the tops of which were still covered by snow.

Loud voices and trampling on the deck indicated that the cutter had reached its destination. It was evening and there were a few people standing along the riverbank with nets over their heads. Planks were placed from the boat to the shore and all were ordered off. People tottered down the makeshift gangplank and had to be careful not to fall carrying their sad collection of clothes. They were greeted by swarms of mosquitoes and moskas - biting flies, which soon ate Janis' forehead raw and he pulled his cap down to make some protection. The moskas crawled up his arms and into his eyes and mouth. When he bit down on one, it tasted sweet and of blood. The new arrivals soon found that it was necessary to wash the exposed flesh that was covered in red marks or the constant scratching easily turned into nasty boils.

When the unloading was finished the cutter, with its rattling motor, pulled away leaving a bleary eyed small group standing forlornly on the riverbank now facing an ever more uncertain future. Someone started to sing *Dievs Sveti Latvija,* God Bless Latvia to help console the group and then everyone joined in. Janis felt an incredibly long way from home and had never felt more afraid. Eventually the group picked up their battered suitcases and bundles of clothes and started up the riverbank towards a village higher up. The first wooden house they came to was abandoned and had empty holes instead of glass windows.

The Latvians and Volga Germans decided to make the

beaten up and abandoned house their home. It was quite large and was divided into two sections. The Latvians took one section and the Volga Germans the other. There was no furniture. Grass was gathered and they used this as bedding for their first night. The next day the planks used to disembark from the cutter, which had been left on the bank, were cut up to make benches that could also be used to sleep on.

Sleeping for some was difficult. The constant sunlight streamed in the windows and they were all plagued with bed bugs. The bugs had somehow survived since the last inhabitants deserted the house. Now they were flat, transparent and as ravenous as wolves.

Janis found that, with their arrival, there were twenty Latvians in total in the village comprising six teenagers and fourteen women. There was a similar number of Volga Germans and there were men included in this number.

Janis and some of the teenage boys set about exploring the wild but beautiful landscape. The warmth of the sun, nature and the allure of a teenage girl named Juta, who had settled in his house with her mother, helped to lessen a deep and persistent anxiety.

Fishing

After a few days of being left alone, the newly arrived group had their first visitor. About ten kilometres north from the village was a collective farm and from there arrived its Chairman together with two female representatives. The inhabitants from a variety of houses were marshalled together and then taken to a nearby village, Plahina, by boat. Plahina had about forty houses, a grain store, a community hall, a tiny school and a small, poorly-provisioned shop. The group travelled a little further to a sandy beach-like strip on the bank of the Yenisei and it was from there that fishing was organised. The new recruits were given rudimentary instruction on how to use the large dragnets.

Fishing comprised the daily work of the group. The boats and nets were kept on the sandy beach and every morning the group made the long walk there. The day consisted of throwing a long net into the river, dragging it along for some way and then pulling it into a boat. Very quickly the boat filled with water. Although the air was warm the river water felt icy and to save their footwear the fisher folk only had bare feet. To get the boat back to the shore Janis had to jump in up to his waist and drag the boat over the rocks that were scattered along the riverbank. It took him some time to warm up again. Despite the exertion, initially the dragnet remained empty.

As the days passed the fisher folk started to catch some fish. The most common type was sturgeon and this commanded the best price. For the whole catch the group were paid a few roubles and given a limited number of food stamps. The stamps only provided the right to buy food but there was never enough money or sufficient available food to live on. The only way to survive was to keep back some of their catch. Soon an order was issued mandating that only 200g of fish per person per day was allowed to be kept and a policeman was allocated to ensure that the rule was maintained. Luckily for the group the policeman was also a drinker and his checking was not very diligent. Without the extra allocation it was clear that they would starve.

Occasionally Janis would look over to Sonja who worked as hard as the rest pulling in the nets. He was amazed at her strength considering how petite she was. Her hands were not like those of the other women, especially those who came from farming stock. She had slender fingers. It hurt Janis to see his mother's hand badly chapped at the end of the day. Occasionally he asked her whether she would like him to drip the paraffin wax of a candle onto her cracked skin. She always refused but for Janis it provided temporary relief.

Janis began to learn a little more about the history of the local inhabitants. All were Russian but most of the ancestors came from far away. Some were descended from 'old believers' who had been persecuted under tsarist times. Some were from settlers who had willingly arrived to find a life that was not under control of the landed gentry. Another group were the Russian 'kulaks' who had been deported in the thirties. The kulaks were a special group of people who did not work for the collective farm. They were the deported farm owners who had decided not to give up on their industrious ways. They ran independent enterprises with their own boats and fishing gear. The government taxed them heavily and Janis wondered how they managed.

Janis found that the attitude of the locals was mostly friendly and as helpful as their limited resources allowed. Yet they remained distant. Propaganda was powerful and had reached even to the depths of Siberia. Firstly, the new arrivals were foreigners and foreigners, it appeared to Janis, would never be trusted in Russia.

After two weeks of constant work Janis had a day off and he set off with his newly established friend, Harijs, to explore their surrounding area.

Harijs was a year younger than Janis and he lived with his mother and seven other women in a run down wooden house in the settlement. Unlike Janis, Harijs had come from the countryside. His family had a small farm near Salaspils, which was just outside of Riga, and Janis was surprised to learn that the first time Harijs had visited the capital was when he was deported. Although their backgrounds were different, both had adventurous natures.

Janis found that the trees were quite different to those of mid-Siberia. There were no pines but there were a large variety of deciduous trees and a few cedars and white firs. Further north the forest gave way to swamps. The ice had only just melted and Janis was amazed at how everything grew so fast in the warmth and the thick fertile soil.

The explorers turned foragers and one day they went to pick wild rhubarb and onions, which grew in abundance along the riverbank. They returned tired but not entirely happy. The moska, which plagued them all day, had spoiled their fun. It was only when a breeze had sprung up that they had any respite. In the quiet of the evening, as Janis and Harijs counted their bite marks, Sonja said, 'If I ever have the opportunity here to entertain Joseph Vissarionovich Dzhughashvili, our Uncle Stalin, I would tie him to a tree and let the moskas talk to him instead.' Janis and Harijs were at first surprised with such a daring comment and then they burst into laughter.

The summer sunshine was interspersed with the occasional rainy period. During these times the clothes never quite dried despite there being a constantly burning stove in the house. In less than a month a pair of trousers had rotted on Janis.

The sunny weather warmed the river and eventually it was possible to swim in it. The Yenisei was so wide it would have been impossible for the boys to swim to the other side but they went so far that they were out of sight – much to their mothers' worry.

After the ladies had made nets to protect the wearer from the moskas, Janis and his friend Harijs started to collect berries and other wild produce. They found that after the cloudberries came the elderberries, then the loganberries and finally the cranberries. The forest was abundant for a brief period.

By late-August there was a short night. These dark hours were called 'the thieves night' and were used to good effect. Janis and his trusted aides sneaked out and pilfered potatoes from the collective farm.

In the autumn the catch increased and fishing became a twenty-four hour operation, but as time went on the river got colder and colder. Although fishing was best at night, the water in the boat almost froze. At the front of the fishing boat was a brazier with a fire in it to help lure the catfish into the net and it helped to lessen the fisher folks' violent shivering. Unfortunately the old nets often tore and they lost some of the catch. Occasionally, Janis and the others spent the whole day mending the nets and then fishing would resume at night.

Fishing carried on in all weathers. The Chairman of the collective farm walked about in high boots and raincoat but the fisher folk had to tie bits of netting around their feet to keep warm. Janis and the other boys got used to the cold and went about their duties with bare feet. Then, one night, they thought that salt had been spilt on the bank. It was frost and, from then on, they too tied cloth around their feet to keep warm.

The best delicacy was catfish livers, which were quite large. The Russian women showed the new arrivals how to get the liver out without cutting the fish. This involved piercing a hole under the gill and squeezing out the liver. The removed livers were hidden and then taken back to the houses for salting. Stuffing small fish into the empty holes where the livers used to be ensured that the catch passed inspection.

The livers together with other stolen fish were salted and put in boxes after they had dried out. By the end of the season Janis' household had salted over forty kilograms of fish and they hoped that this would see them through the winter ahead.

One night Janis and Harijs were walking back to their houses from the fishing grounds. As they passed through a shadow of the trees created by the bright moonlight they could see ahead a silhouetted figure hanging about Janis' house. They quickly and quietly took cover in the nearby bushes. As the figure approached he stopped opposite the bush and took his rifle off his shoulder. The boys did not dare breath and thought that the man, whom they recognised as the Chairman of the collective farm, must have spotted them. Then he placed his rifle down, unbuttoned his flies and relieved himself in front of the onlooking boys.

It was clear that the Chairman had been snooping around and the boys reported this to the household. It was agreed that in the morning they would find a safe place in the forest to store the stolen fish. However, before light the Chairman returned with the policeman and the hoard of fish was seized. Janis was ordered to take the fish to the boat and when he returned the women were in tears. His mother explained, 'Ziga has been arrested as the main thief and Jana has been arrested as her accomplice.' Janis could not believe how arbitrary the selection had been. He suddenly felt scared and vulnerable. He wanted to shout and scream that such selection was unfair but he knew that this would make things worse.

Later in the month there was a trial. The main 'thief' and her 'accomplice' were found guilty of stealing food that was meant for workers and were both sentenced to five years in prison. They were taken away and Janis was never to see them again. He felt hopeless and at the same time relieved that it was not his mother who had been sent away.

In a reversal of fortune Janis heard later that the Chairman had had his hut searched and it was found to contain boxes of the best fish. It was clear to Janis that the Chairman had failed to share his 'catch' with his superiors and paid the price with a ten-year sentence.

Article 58

Winter in the Far North

Day by day the temperature fell and the wind increased but it was rarely cold enough for the fishing to stop. The rules were that if a jug of water was thrown and it froze in mid air or eyelids froze to the cheek, then fishing could be suspended for a short while. Often the wind blew in wet snow. The fisher folk shivered and shook but kept on fishing. Eventually some footwear was provided. Janis was given a pair of boots made of tarpaulin with wooden soles, which proved to be highly dangerous as they slipped easily on the wet, wooden decks. Janis banged some nails into the sole of the boots but this acted to build up a huge layer of snow when he was out of the boat and, as such, walking proved difficult.

Autumn turned into winter and the fishing continued. The fisher folk had to walk through the snow to the boats and then wade through the icy sludge at the riverbank to launch the vessels. The frozen nets would only thaw when immersed into the river. The soupy water soon turned into unbreakable ice at the margins of the river and then the boats could not be launched. The exhausted group were given some time off before receiving new orders, and this period of rest enabled Sonja and the other women in the house to make something in the way of winter clothing out of the remaining rags.

When fishing with the dragnets ceased, Janis set

about berry picking. The redcurrants had turned quite sweet in the frost and ice and even the orange berries of the mountain ash were edible.

The night time's entertainments were the northern lights. The eerie waving pulses covered the whole sky. Sometimes they ebbed and then built again into a peak. One evening when Janis and Harijs were returning from their duties the waving was particularly active. Curtains of green and red light pulsed across the night sky. Harijs asked Janis, 'Do you think that these lights are trying to send a message or say something?' Janis briefly thought about the question and answered, 'Why are you here?'

Only the strong wind kept the whole river from freezing. Then, on the first windless night, it froze over. However, for a time the ice was thin enough to be broken by the occasional passing ship. When it froze into an impenetrable plate the ice was full of jagged edges. Some of these looked like panes of glass and, in fact, some of the locals cut them off to use as makeshift storm windows. When ice fishing started, Janis and the others could feel the ice swaying but this gradually reduced as the depth of the ice increased to over two metres.

As the catches were very small some of the Volga Germans and a few others, including Janis and Harijs, were ordered to go further up the Yenisei where it was reported that fish were still being caught in large numbers. The group were given fur coats, thick boots and skis and had to carry all their tackle and tents on their backs. They had walked quite a way on skis when a Purga, a Siberian snowstorm, suddenly blew in. This was unusual in that it was so early on in the season.

In an instant the wind began a wild and terrifying howling that, at first, forced everyone to squat on the ground. Then there was a tremendous clap of thunder and a violent stream of snow and ice particles were whipped at their faces. The force of the wind and the plummeting temperature made it hard to breathe. Everyone roped themselves together and turned back. The wind was so strong it created a terrible groaning sound from the stovepipe that one man was carrying. They lent into the wind and stumbled onwards but could not see more than a metre in front of them. The pace slowed as the wind increased and the icy crystals stung their eyes.

The weight on Janis' back seemed to get heavier with every step and he suddenly felt the need to rest. 'Stop,' he shouted but the wind whipped the word away. He knelt down and then experienced a beautiful feeling of calm. Everything turned rose coloured. Harijs slapping his face cut his reverie short and he got up and staggered on into the biting wind. Then, after slipping and sliding up a steep path, Janis collapsed in front of a door where Sonja huddled waiting anxiously for her son's return.

Janis was in bed for two days after this but apart from frozen cheeks that first turned black and then recovered there was no lasting damage. The fishing expedition had been a failure and was rewarded with the coats, boots and skis being taken back.

Janis' duties turned from fishing to hunting. He and

his friend Harijs were given twenty big traps and forty small ones but no training on how to use them. The fur receiver was supposed to give some instruction but was dismissive of the boys. The existing hunters were not prepared to reveal their secrets and increase the competition for the available furs.

As it turned out, the Volga German men knew something of hunting and through a slow process of communication in Russian, Janis and Harijs managed to pick up rudimentary principles. The first successful catch took some time to come but both boys were delighted when they returned to a trap to find a big white hare in it. They felt like mighty hunters bringing back their first game and were greeted with cheers of delight when this was placed on the table. Janis looked over to Juta whom he had become fond of and he knew that she was proud of him.

As was the case with the fish, all the hunted animals were supposed to go to the collective farm but this hare was kept for themselves. Once it had been prepared, slowly cooked and eaten Janis thought, 'Was there ever such a tasty meal?'

The deep snow meant that the hunters really needed skis and Janis set about making a pair from old fence panels that had escaped being used as firewood. With simple tools he fashioned a pair of skis. At first they were just thin planks tied to boots. As initially there was no curve at the end, the planks occasionally cut into the snow and Janis would topple over headfirst. The first version became known as 'The Snow Inspectors' on account that the wearer would often end up looking in close-up at the snow crystals. Over time, and with constant modification, including soaking the wood to create a bend in the tip, the skis worked remarkably well.

Janis provided Harijs with a pair of homemade skis and by being able to roam over a large area the boys became increasingly successful hunters. They were especially good at trapping hares. They camouflaged the traps and rubbed pine needles onto them to wipe away the smell of metal. Yet, they found that they could not catch anything with the smaller traps despite putting them along the tracks of small animals.

When the temperature made a sudden fall, and the extreme snowstorm of a Purga blew up, Janis and Harijs lost half their traps. They had not properly marked where they had put them and after the Purga everywhere looked different as the snow was so much thicker. They were informed that the lost traps would be added to their mounting debt that accumulated as more equipment, such as the fishing nets, was either lost or broken.

During the Purga the wind penetrated the thickest of walls and the poor Russian stove was not up to the job of heating the whole room. The benefit of the cold was that the bed bugs stopped biting and there were other recompenses. Hare meat was plentiful and they ate well whilst the Purga did its worst outside. Inside, Janis was with the two women that he loved looking after, his mother and Juta.

With the wind howling outside, Janis and the others in the house would gather closely around the stove and tell stories that they knew. When their memories failed they filled in with the fruits of their own imagination. One night Janis and Juta were left sitting by the stove after the story telling. They sat closely to each other and he felt Juta breathing gently. After a period of listening to the noises outside, they pondered on whether they would ever see their home country again. Juta whispered, 'I don't care as long as I'm with you.' Janis had never felt happier.

In the morning Janis slept until late in the morning. The wind had eased but it was still dark when he got up. Juta had been sent to fetch water and her mother approached Janis. 'Don't think that I am blind to what is going on between you two,' she whispered, 'don't go too far. I want you to give me your word that you won't...won't take advantage.' At first Janis was unsure quite what she was saying but then coloured deeply in embarrassment. 'Of course not, I promise,' he uttered.

Gradually Janis and Harijs were able to find their way about the tundra and taiga despite it being disorientating in the snow. They began to enjoy the polar nights. Under the northern lights, and in the deafening silence after the Purga, they resumed their stealthy work as hunters. Once, and only once, they caught a fox. They were proud of their achievement, as they were the first in the village to catch one that season. They did not confess that the fox must have accidentally fallen into the trap set for hares. They earned 80 roubles and wished that they had caught a blue fox as that would have earned them 1000 roubles.

One evening Janis was sitting in the house with the others when there was a knock at the door. A tall thin man wearing a coat that was too lightweight for the season stood there and asked for accommodation. There was something trustworthy about his face that made the woman agree to put him up for the night. He was almost blown in by the strong wind outside. The stranger was offered something to eat and the opportunity to warm himself as best he could by the stove. He had walked from the Gulag at Norilska and spoke Russian. Janis was able to follow most of what the man said about his life.

The houseguest for the night told the group that he

had been deported from Leningrad in 1937 and now must return. He was part of a large workforce of forced labour that was involved in logging in the Far North. The man told that he had escaped and had managed to dodge the guards. Now he had to be careful, as he knew that it was not the guards that were most dangerous. Siberians had been told that there was a bounty on the head of any prisoner killed whilst on the run.

In the morning and still under the cover of darkness the stranger set off into the taiga with no means of telling the direction apart from the vast starry sky. Janis knew that he walked to a certain death. 'Nature and the weather are too wild for such a crazy venture,' he thought and then pondered on what life must be like in the Gulag for the man to risk escape, or what was so important that he was prepared to walk thousands of kilometres for.

With the permanent nights, it was easy to lose track of dates and by midwinter it was not possible to be sure when Christmas Day was. If they ever managed to see a newspaper it was a big occasion but it was always months out of date. These papers were thoroughly read and discussed but they did not help with keeping up with the calendar. Janis and all the inhabitants decided that they would have their Christmas meal during the next Purga. They joked that this year they would not have the traditional pork but would rather have hare. When the Purga blew up they had the dinner and after that they sang their favourite carols in the comfort of knowing that their voices would be carried away on the winds of the Purga and that no one would report them for

Article 58

celebrating Christmas.

Article 58

Spring 1943

Janis and Sonja had somehow survived another Siberian winter and the end of the really cold days brought changes. Janis and Harijs were told that there was no profit in their hunting and that Janis and his mother were to be transferred to fishing duties in the lakes further north. The lakes were ominously named The Plague Lakes and were on the other side of the Yenesei.

Janis' first action was to find out whether Juta and Harijs had also been transferred. Harijs and his mother had received similar orders but Juta had heard nothing and in the short time given to Janis and Sonja to prepare for their departure, no such instruction came. On the day of leaving there were many tears shed. Separation was becoming more difficult as time went on, not easier. To make it possible to leave they all believed that they would be transferred further north soon enough. Juta suggested to the boys, 'Let's have a midsummer party when we are reunited.' It was physical pain that Janis felt as he started his journey north. He was never to see Juta again.

A young village lad, who drove the cart carrying the rags that now amounted to the deportees' worldly possessions, escorted the small group of transferees. He had been allocated an old hunting rifle but this was often left unattended at the back of the cart.

Whilst walking through the taiga Janis commented to his mother, 'Security doesn't need to be tight as the real guard is the taiga itself. Who can live alone here? The locals can smell a stranger twenty kilometres away.'

Walking was hard as the ground was still frozen and the reflected sunlight from ice and snow was blindingly bright even though they walked through the forest. The only sign of life was high in the treetops where the breeze blew and the twitter of birds could be heard. In the warmth of midday the occasional squirrel that had ventured from its hibernation could be seen leaping from branch to branch. Once in a birch grove they saw a long-nosed elk, which vanished with a faint crackle of twigs under the ice. Ahead stretched a continual scene of ridges, dips and exposed roots.

The beauty of walking through the pristine wilderness did nothing to lift Janis' sense of foreboding. He felt suffocated despite breathing in invigorating air. He still had no news about his father and as he looked at his mother his worst fears about her came to him. Sonja had turned forty five during the winter and that seemed to be incredibly old to him. 'How much more can Mamma take?' he thought and then realised just how worried he was about being left to face Siberia alone.

They walked in silence and occasionally from the top of a ridge they could see snow-covered mountaintops in the distance. Night time was spent huddled in a very dilapidated hut. It was a tiny structure with smoke-blackened walls and a floor that was scorch-marked by the campfires lit there in winter. A bundle of dried twigs lay in one corner, left there by the last inhabitant. It was the custom to leave fuel and matches for the next visitor and, to Janis, this seemed to be a remarkable act of kindness given what he had seen so far of how people considered the welfare of their fellow man. In the middle of the roof there was only a small opening for the smoke to escape. By the morning Janis joked to his mother about being 'kippered' in the night.

Next day they resumed their walk and the path moved from the taiga to the tundra and frozen swamps. Then it crossed frozen lakes. Eventually they came across a small settlement of four huts. In front of one of the huts was a group of women and Janis was amazed that he recognised some of them. He and Sonja had worked with them in the meadows of mid-Siberia. It was a subdued reunion as the women were starving. Fishing provided only a little supplement to a meagre diet. The poor catch had to be sent to the collective farm and all the time the ladies were scared to be caught pilfering.

Janis and Sonja were allocated to what could only be described as a hut. It was made of logs and insulated by peat. The floor was beaten earth and the walls were smoky black. Unusually it had small slits for windows, which cast the interior in perpetual gloom even in the summer. In the winter, the hut became completely dark as the slits were stuffed with more peat to keep in the vestigial heat that radiated from a poor stove. The hut had a pitched roof covered in stones with a tiny vent for the stovepipe to poke through.

Later that day the fishing brigade foreman, Ivan Yakovlevich Velichko, made an appearance. He immediately struck a note of fear into Janis with his slab-like appearance and cold, watery eyes. Janis soon learnt that Velichko's heart and soul ran on plentiful supplies of cheap vodka and he often remained in his cabin for days. When he came out everyone had to be extremely vigilant not to cross the brute. It came as a complete surprise to Janis when he found that one of the prettiest ladies in the Brigade also lived in the cabin with the drunkard.

In the following weeks after his arrival, Janis was taken with the idea that Velichko must have some dreadful hold over the young woman. He could not go to sleep without thinking how he might save the damsel from her torment. He thought how much of a hero he would be and how he would be rewarded for his efforts.

Janis discovered that there is a distinct and prolonged fifth season in the Far North. There is a time when winter is over but spring has yet to arrive. The nights are freezing cold and the days are full of warm sunshine. In the very earliest part of this season at the settlement the only living things seemed to be the sad inhabitants and the plentiful lice.

In the morning sun the sad and hungry fisher folk mended nets and made new ones. Floats made of birch bark kept these up and stones tied to the bottom helped the nets sink. Despite the use of dozens of nets few fish were caught.

In the middle of the fifth season, when the sun had

real power in it and hibernating bears were stirring, Velichko came out of his vodka lair for longer periods. He would check the fish and search around for any signs of pilfering. Expletives followed him around like a bad odour.

One grey and chilly afternoon Janis had the opportunity to free the damsel from the clutches of the satanic Velichko.

Powered or numbed by the plentiful intake of vodka, Velichko unusually demanded that Janis accompany him to bring some netting back from the fishing holes on the still frozen lake. Janis was not happy about undertaking the duty. Not only did he hate the sight of Velichko, the ice had started to creek whenever anyone walked on it. He carried with him a large stick to tap on the ice ahead to ensure that it was safe.

Velichko was a big man but for some reason the ice was silent when they ventured onto it. Then, someway onto the lake and without warning, it gave way. Velichko suddenly disappeared leaving Janis standing only two metres away. For a moment there was utter silence. Velichko's head reappeared along with a dreadful roar as he gasped against the cold of the water.

Janis saw that about ten metres away was some netting and he knew this could be used to haul Velichko out without getting too close to the new hole. However, he hesitated and the world went into slow motion. Seconds seemed to be like hours as he wrestled with his thoughts. Velichko had got his arms onto the side of the ice hole and was about to haul himself onto the edge when Janis raised his stick and brought it down as hard as he could on the top of his head. Velichko's face was contorted with pain, cold and hatred and this was Janis' last image of the man as he slumped into the icy water. Treading as gently as he could, Janis walked back with a sense of elation to the settlement to report the dreadful accident.

Janis told everyone what had happened. Velichko had fallen in and he had tried to save him with the netting but Velichko must have been too big or weak to haul himself out of the water. He vowed at that point never to say anything different to anyone, not even his mother.

That night the bubble of elation burst. A sense of achievement was replaced with a feeling of dread. Janis could not believe what he had done and asked himself, 'Where did that anger come from? I hardly knew Velichko. What harm had he done to me?' There was no sleep to be had that night. The memory of Velichko's growl and the sight of his face prevented any rest.

The next day Janis was surprised that Velichko's 'widow' did not rejoin the other ladies now freed from the clutches of the foreman. Then, he was told that Velichko was cheating the rest of the women. He used their food stamps to keep his mistress fed. Finding out that the harlot had chosen her prison felt like he had been thrown into the icy lake. He shivered now with the thought that an investigation would show that he murdered the foreman. Again, sleep was in short supply.

Janis thought about his father and what he might say if he found out about his son being a killer. He felt connected to him more now than ever before but contrasted his father's actions to that of his own, 'I killed Velichko because I was a coward. Pappa killed the enemy because he was a hero.'

As the fifth season moved on birch sap collected from the nearby trees foretold the return of life to this once desolate scene. The lakes remained covered in ice until early June and the first signs of spring came from under the remains of the snow on the lakeside. Then the green shoots of new life broke through what looked like scorched grass. In the twilight the voices of returning swans could be heard and the occasional prints of an awakened bear were seen in the remaining snow. In the sun the temperature rose but when a cloud passed overhead winter briefly returned. With a sudden cold spell the returning migrants risked starvation and the swans hit their bellies as they landed heavily on the newly reformed transparent ice covering the lake.

The fisher folk clung to the margins of life and felt as vulnerable as the returning birds.

When the ice had melted Harijs discovered Velichko on the lakeside. Janis feigned an illness and remained in his hut until the body had been buried.

A bonfire had to be kept alight all day so that the ground was soft enough for them to dig a grave. A simple larch cross marked the spot where Velichko's body was laid to rest. The backdrop was a spectacular view of lakes and mountains, which Janis thought could make a scene for a picture postcard but would never write to anyone, 'Wish you were here'.

To Janis' relief there was no investigation into the death. Velichko was too far away and too unloved it seemed for anyone to mount such a thing. The administration simply sent a replacement.

Harijs' Fateful Trip

The new foreman, Kolodin, was the exact opposite of Velichko. He was tall and thin, even gaunt and kept himself to himself. He was too old to be called up to the army but no one knew anything about the man's history and how come he had ended up by the lakes. What they did find out was that he was a great boat builder. Janis and Harijs at first watched him go about his trade. They saw how he used an axe to fashion the bottom of a boat out of a large cedar log. Having completed the boat it needed to be made watertight and Kolodin sealed it using melted resin scraped off the larch trees. Then over the course of the short summer Kolodin taught the boys how to use an axe so that they too eventually could fashion wood in a similar way. Even though they worked together Kolodin never asked any questions of the boys or gave away any detail about himself.

Around midsummer there was enough open water to put out the dragnets and suddenly the fish arrived. There were so many that the water seemed to boil. The sudden change in diet had a dramatic impact. Spirits rose but some were cut down by acute diarrhoea. Everyone was angry that a supply of simple medicine would have prevented the unnecessary suffering.

Janis thought of Juta. They had hoped to meet up at midsummer's eve, but he would not inflict this wonderful but harsh place on anyone.

The summer came and the lakes turned warm. With the warmth came the moskas and they returned with a vengeance. The only way to survive was to cover up with nets. However, when a gentle breeze set in the moskas disappeared and the women would don homemade swimming costumes. Janis was proud of his slender looking mother. Kolodin looked on without any apparent interest.

Fishing started early in the morning with the dragnets first being loaded onto the boats. By noon with a large catch on board the group would come ashore for lunch. A bonfire was lit and fish soup was cooked. Every time Janis used to say, 'This is better than in the best restaurants in Moscow', and the retort would always be, 'And better service too.'

Later in the summer the daily catch began to fall away and an official arrived to ensure that the people worked more and rested less. But even the might of the Soviet authority could not summon the fish into the nets.

The short summer quickly gave way to autumn and before too long the lakes began to freeze over. At first it was possible to break the ice with oars although the sharp fragments would often tear the nets. When the ice was too thick the standing nets were deployed through holes in the surface. The stock of fish dwindled and a longer and longer distance between the ice holes had to be covered. Janis used his previous experience and his recently acquired skill with an axe to good effect and made everyone a pair of skis.

There were about twenty people in Janis' fishing brigade consisting mainly of intelligent, well-educated women. As such, Janis' education continued through the winter months. As a pupil at school he had been bright and diligent and here too he was thirsty for knowledge. In the evening the ladies would retell stories from the great literature that they knew and one of the ladies who spoke Russian fluently tutored Janis in the language.

Starvation crept slowly upon them. The desire for food was the primitive instinct around which mental life centred. In the first months, cooking and recipes became the most popular topic. Sonja had the widest knowledge of cooking but it was almost impossible for Janis to listen to his mother recount her recipes. It reminded him of the times when his parents gave rather lavish dinner parties. He was packed off to bed after the guests had arrived but he was able to see the lovely laid table. From his bedroom Janis listened to the tinkle of glasses and cutlery on the fine bone china plates and went to sleep to the sound of laughter.

At the start of the working day, Janis was given a small amount of bread and he would tenderly touch this in his coat pocket and stroke it with frozen, gloveless fingers. Then he would break off a crumb and put this in his mouth. With the last bit of willpower he would put the rest back into his pocket having promised himself that he would hold out until the afternoon.

After the daily duties, discussions would immediately start on food. The same question was repeated over and over, 'What is your favourite recipe?' Regularly, each of the inhabitants would plan a menu for when there was a reunion; the day in the distant future after they had been liberated and sent home. Janis kept reviewing his menu and eventually settled on beetroot soup followed by goose stuffed with sauerkraut. Pickled pumpkins, mushrooms and gherkins would accompany this. As a dessert he would have 'floating islands', which consisted of whipped egg whites boiled in milk and placed in a cranberry sauce. However, as soon as he had settled on this and recounted it to the others in the hut, he could almost smell duck fat roasting in the oven. In the morning the menu had changed to include roasted duck stuffed with apples followed by klingeris cake.

Mentally rehearsing the fine dining to come only heightened the hunger pangs. When the last layers of subcutaneous fat had vanished, all the inhabitants began to look like skeletons disguised with skin and rags. During the daily search for lice Janis studied his body and would often think, 'What has become of me? My body is digesting my muscles. Is this what a corpse looks like?'

Janis tried to force himself to think of things other than food and often would consider questions such as what branch of medicine he would take up when back in Riga. However, it was not long before his imagination had worked in a food angle. For instance, he would be a doctor in the hospital but one who was sitting in the canteen enjoying a good lunch.

The reality of the diet was a very watery soup and bread that was made out of a meagre supply of flour, sugar and margarine that had to be brought in from a collection point every two weeks.

A rota system was established for the collection duties. Janis and Sonja were the ones rostered from their hut to make the journey and Harijs and his mother were the ones from their hut. In the summer the round trip was a relatively short journey. In the depths of the winter it was an altogether different story; it only became semi-light between noon and two 'o' clock and the temperature could be as low as - 40°C.

On the 30th January 1945 it was Harijs and his mother's turn to make the trip. On the way a Purga blew in. Janis and Sonja realised that this could be very serious but they were unable to do anything, as they knew that if they went outside they would not see more than a hand in front. All they could do was wait. The next day Harijs miraculously returned but alone.

Janis helped his friend to his hut and all the ladies there made him as warm as they could. Janis stayed with Harijs continuously through two nights and listened to his horrific story. With tears running down his cheeks and mouthing 'Mamma,' over and over again, Harijs gave in to his frostbite and died.

Janis felt desolate. For a few days he did not get up and then with gentle encouragement from Sonja he started to go about his normal activities.

During the winter, a Regional Officer visited occasionally. He was fit and large as a bull and somehow had escaped the call up of the army. He arrived once whilst the women were singing a traditional Latvian song, *Tautiešami Roku Devu* and demanded to know what they were singing, clearly concerned that the lyrics told of some revolutionary tale. He seemed less than convinced when he was told that the song was about how a girl gave her hand to a young boy.

Later, the Regional Officer asked Janis to accompany him on a walk into the forest. After a short while the man stopped, lit a cigarette and offered one to Janis. Talking slowly he promised Janis the opportunity to return to Latvia if he would inform on the activities of the group. Whilst he talked with a smile, his right hand unbuttoned the holster of the pistol he was carrying. Janis was clear about the proposition but pretended that his Russian was poor and did not understand what was being put to him. Then his nerve failed and he turned and fled as past as he could. At any moment he expected a bullet to cut him down.

Janis reached his hut drenched in sweat and told everything that had just happened. The ladies were very supportive and told how they too had been approached to be an informer. It was clear then to him that mutual spying and betraying was pretty much the common practice in Soviet Russia.

News of the end of the Second World War reached the Brigade at the end of May 1945. This was not greeted with jubilation as it truly meant that the deportees would remain enemies of the people. Yet there was hope that something would change. The day after hearing the news Janis said to his mother, 'Surely our work of providing rations will soon be over.' His mother's reply was not as positive as he had thought that it might be, 'Well, we can only wait and see.' Despite Janis' hopes, there was no immediate change to the regime and fishing continued although the catches dwindled.

Article 58

The Accident

The winter of 1945/1946 that the Brigade spent at the lakes was the hardest. Fish had been in short supply all summer and the meagre rations meant that starvation again threatened. With the lack of food the winter ailments seemed to be worse. Frozen cheeks turned into black scabs and boils erupted leaving behind blue marks. Janis heard of ladies in a nearby settlement whose teeth hurt and then simply fell out. Yet, despite all of the deprivation, it was amazing to him that people rarely caught colds. This was despite often returning home soaked in freezing water. If a cold did come, it passed as quickly as it came.

Without much changing, life continued through two more summers. The major incident of the last summer at the lakes was the suicide of Velichko's widowed mistress. She had moved to a new fishing brigade but her past meant that no one talked to her. Siberia was cold and lonely enough without the icy isolation from your compatriots. With this news, Velichko again visited Janis of a night. He could see his white face and the huge arm that extended to grab him and he sometimes woke the other people in the hut by calling, 'No, Velichko no.'

Janis continued to learn from the ladies and in the really long and quiet days of winter, when there was rest, he would play the harmonica and the others would hum or sing along. When not playing, he analysed the music and its patterns to try to understand why Latvian folk songs were so appealing.

In the autumn of 1947 Janis was ordered to accompany a Finnish man named Pauli who was charged with finding new fishing grounds further north. Pauli was an older man of around fifty years of age who was short but powerfully built. He had been deported from the Finnish border area in 1939.

Janis had become proficient enough in Russian to have interesting conversations with Pauli and he soon found out that he had been moved with his family to live in a settlement about an hour's walk further north. He also found out that he was the father of five children, all girls, and that he lived with four of them in a hut together with another family. Just as with Janis' sister, Pauli's oldest girl had been living away from home when the Russian Army herded the rest of the family into canvas-covered trucks and out of their country. His wife had died of septicemia in giving birth to their last child.

The lakes for which they searched were supposed to be somewhere at the foot of the Haitika Mountains. They travelled by foot without maps or compasses for such things were classified as spying devices. Pauli proved to be a good navigator and Janis was sure that they would find the lakes. They walked for several days towards the east through tundra and swamps, sometimes wading up to their knees in water. In the swamps each carried a stick and they tied themselves together on a long rope just in case one fell into a bog. At night they found firm ground and hunkered down under a stretched-out piece of canvas.

Janis and Pauli talked of their experiences in Siberia and at the end of this Janis was sure that, by comparison, he had had quite an easy time of it. For two years Pauli had the worst job in the world, it seemed to Janis. This had involved working in a tar facility. Pauli explained that tar and turpentine were extracted from highly resinous trees by effectively boiling them up in huge vats, which were heated by burning logs under them. Tar flowed from one end of the vat and turpentine from the other. It was hot and poisonous work and Pauli had only been released from this because the work was given to a contingent of *zeks* - prisoners.

Just before Janis and Pauli went to sleep on the second night Pauli asked, 'Do you believe in God?' Janis' first thought was, 'How strange it is that I have never before been asked this.' After a brief hesitation Janis replied, 'Sometimes.' What he wanted to say was, 'Sometimes I do, then I remember that I killed a man and wonder how God will choose to punish me. I sleep better by not believing in God.' No more questions were asked on the subject but just before sleep overcame Janis, he looked over towards his companion, and in the moonlight, he could just make out that Pauli was lying with his hands together in prayer.

On the third day Janis and Pauli walked through a larch forest in the late afternoon and had to cross a deep gully. Rather than walk down and through a boggy looking stream they decided to cross over a fallen tree that conveniently formed a bridge. Pauli went first and had barely reached the other side when he heard a snap that sounded as loud as a gun shot in the silence of the forest. Janis had slipped off the trunk and his left leg had caught in a forked branch at the side. The lateral forces snapped his shin as if it was a twig. Janis' lower leg was now at a severely distorted angle and his face was contorted in pain. The pain became so severe that for a time he passed out and woke up only when Pauli had managed somehow to unhook his leg and drag him back to the mossy cover on the forest floor. They both realised the seriousness of the situation. Janis' shin was splintered and parts of the bone threatened to poke through the skin.

Firstly, Pauli made a fire and then cut down small larch trees. Using a small branch he tied a splint to Janis' leg. Again, Janis felt himself go woozy with the pain. Every small movement sent what seemed like a lightning bolt of electricity into his leg, which travelled up his body so that he saw flashes of light.

After a relatively short time Pauli had used the canvas, which they carried with them, and larch branches to construct a makeshift stretcher. By then though it was getting dark and they rested as best they could by the fire until dawn. Janis hardly slept with the thudding and incessant pain. In the early dawn he heard the voices of distant swans, presumably on the lakes that they so nearly found. It was strange to hear them as most had long gone with the approach of winter. Janis thought that a pair would be trying to get their young to fly west. However, the cygnets must have been born too late in the season and with the onset of winter they were all about to perish. Janis knew that the parents never leave their offspring. He felt as helpless as the young swans.

Pauli set off pulling Janis who was strapped to the stretcher; one end of which dragged across the ground. It was painful and slow progress. Janis doubted that one man could pull a person the distance it had taken two fit people to walk in three days. Little by little, jolt after jolt, the stretcher was dragged towards home. At the end of the first day, Pauli made a fire, collected berries and mushrooms and went to sleep for a solid eight hours. Janis hardly slept as the smallest of movements made it feel like hot pins were being inserted slowly into his leg. The next day, Janis said to Pauli, 'I must try to walk today, you are going to kill yourself pulling me so far,' but he knew that he could put no weight on his leg. Pauli anyway would not hear of testing the possibility.

The drag continued with Pauli resting for longer and longer periods between the hauls. Mostly the mossy ground meant that the bumps were cushioned but even so, some created a jolt that left Janis grunting and clenching his fist. He did everything he could not to show to Pauli just how much pain he was in.

Janis remembered the first two days and then fell into a half-asleep half-awake coma. He dreamed of being back in Riga.

In his reverie, Janis went back to the beginning of the school year after the Soviet occupation. He remembered that the whole atmosphere had changed since the end of the previous term. Janis was warned that he should not say anything to his fellow pupils about what they discussed at home. He could hear his mother saying, 'Never express an opinion.' This seemed to be eminently sensible advice, as soon after, people started to go missing. The first person that Janis personally knew who vanished was the owner of a nearby hunting weapons store.

Janis remembered how the pupils banded together to raise the Latvian flag on the occasion of Latvian Independence above the school. This act of defiance cost the head teacher his job so all the pupils felt rather bad about what they had done.

Janis remembered going to the *Universalveikails*, the department store in the city centre where his mother bought the best haberdashery and he was able to look at the toys and games that came from around the world. The object of his desire was a big box of Meccano. The shop had made a crane for display and he was fascinated by the potential to realise new and fantastic structures. Yet, he did not press his father too hard for this toy as the writing on the box was in a foreign language and he was unsure that he would understand any of the instructions. Then he remembered that after the occupation, this palace of a department store was turned into a place that sold meat and basic products only. Then he imagined he was there in front of the fat Russian women cutting slabs of meat. The voice of one women who had addressed him once returned with every lurch of the stretcher on the ground, 'Speak Russian, speak Russian, speak....'

At one point Janis shouted out, 'No Velichko, no.' He saw the hand of the dead foreman suddenly in front of him. By moving his head to the side Janis managed to avoid Velichko's lunge at his throat. Then he drifted off into a coma of pain, hunger and dreadful fatigue.

Article 58

Hilkka

After six days Pauli had dragged Janis, lungful by lungful of burning breath, to the banks of the Yenisei and there they managed to attract a passing vessel.

Janis was taken to what was known as Grandmother Metusiha's house. She was a large woman who wore a patterned headscarf and a loose shawl that concealed a crippled arm. She gave Janis something to drink that tasted bitter and made him wretch. Then she set to work on his leg. For a long time she used one powerful hand to knead the fractured bone whilst she murmured something over it. Finally, the old woman used dried birch bark to pack around the leg and tied it into place as a caste.

Janis remembered little of the following days. He had a fever and sweated profusely. Often he shouted out in delirium. After five days the fever passed and he woke to the sight of the most beautiful face that he had ever seen. A round faced girl with very blonde hair and piercingly blue eyes looked at him. To Janis, awakening from his ordeal, she seemed like an angel.

At first Janis did not know where he was and why he was in a strange house. Then he recalled the accident. His first words were, 'How is Pauli?' He was fearful that Pauli could have died of exhaustion in dragging a body for so many kilometres. The angel looked confused and then Janis asked the question again but this time in Russian. In a heavily accented Russian, the angel replied, 'He is fine. He slept for two days but is fine now.' He knew then that this beautiful young woman must be one of Pauli's daughters.

There was a knock at the door and in came Sonja, 'Jani, my dear, you are awake.' Janis rose unsteadily on his elbows and tried to sit up straight to receive his mother's hug. He felt under the covers for his bandaged leg and Sonja said, 'You must stay in bed and rest – Grandmother's orders'. Janis had only a vague recollection of what had happened in the old lady's house.

Sonja introduced the angel as Hilkka, one of Pauli's daughters. Her Finnish ancestry was clear. Sonja said in Russian so that Hilkka would understand, 'Hilkka has looked after you since your return'. Hilkka added, 'He has been a good patient' and his mother smiled and said, 'Yes, so far.'

Sonja settled on Janis' bedside whilst Hilkka busied herself elsewhere. He tried to tell what had happened on the expedition but apart from the accident itself the rest of it was hazy. All he could say was, 'I owe my life to Pauli'. His mother confirmed that Pauli had been solidly asleep for almost eighteen hours and had not been able to get out of bed for two days when he returned, but had now resumed his work.

Janis was told that as Pauli was one of the few people in the settlement to have a bed of sorts, he was brought to his house and was now a patient there. To Janis, the lumpy old horsehair mattress was as comfortable as anything to be found in the best of hospitals. 'Will I ever be able to repay Pauli for this?' he thought. Pauli's hut was large and had been divided by the clever use of screens made of reeds into 'rooms' that gave the girls and the other family some privacy.

Janis and his mother chatted for a short while about what was happening in their house. Sonja said that the other women were keen to start spiritualist practice. 'They are desperate to find out if their husbands are alive and if they are dead they want to have a last word with them,' she reported. Continuing she talked about her husband, 'Of course, I want to know what has happened to Reinis but I am against the idea of this spiritualism.'

With the mention of his father, Janis asked his mother a question that he had previously held back, 'Mamma, do you think that Pappa has survived his terrible ordeal?' Sonja looked at Janis for a while and then said gently, 'I don't know whether Pappa is alive or not but at this moment it ceases to matter. Really, nothing could touch the strength of my love, my thoughts and the image of my beloved. Even if Pappa has not survived this hardship, I find strength in his image and my mental conversations are just as satisfying. My love is stronger than death. Anyway, the most important thing here and now is that you are alive.' Both were silent for a while. Then they talked a little more before Sonja rose to go. 'Sleep now, you look tired,' she said and kissed her son. On the way out she said to Hilkka, 'Thank you, you are a kind young woman.'

After Sonja had departed Hilkka tended Janis, made

sure that he was as comfortable as could be and boiled up some pine needle tea, which seemed to help Janis to sleep for a while. Later, Pauli returned from his duties. Janis felt large tears obscure his vision as he shook the hand of Pauli and thanked him for saving his life. Pauli presented Janis with a crutch that he said would be needed temporarily. Then Janis had the need to use it urgently. He gingerly got out of bed and with the aid of Hilkka and the crutch was able to take the sore but not unduly painful steps to the outside privy.

With the help of Hilkka, Janis gradually began to put weight on his leg. When he did so he found that he was about four centrimetres shorter on one side, which generated a severe limp. Gradually he began to walk with the aid of a stick but he realised that from now on he would be an invalid. Invalids, he knew, were treated as the lowest of the low, worse even than criminals, and he felt very down. As the rains turned to sleet and winter again knocked, Janis felt himself become less communicative and sociable. After thinking that he would bounce back after this adversity, the reality of suddenly being an invalid had begun to make him depressed.

The frequent visits from Sonja did little to lift Janis' spirits.

One evening, whilst Pauli sat by Janis' bedside, Janis asked him, 'How do you keep going? Life does not make sense. All I see is suffering and pain. I know that you pray to God. But what sort of God would allow such a mess?' Pauli remained silent for a while and Janis at first thought that he had offended him, then he said, 'Dostoevsky once wrote, 'There is only one thing that I dread; not to be worthy of my sufferings'.' Janis frowned and said, 'I think that I will need your help to understand what is meant by this.'

Pauli spoke quietly and authoritatively, 'The way that you bear your suffering is an inner achievement. It is the spiritual freedom that cannot be taken away. It makes life meaningful and purposeful.' As he had not intended to give a lecture, he paused. Janis thought about what had been said and then replied, 'But my life would be meaningful if I had been able to pursue my career in medicine. As it stands, I have been robbed of this and my physical health.'

Pauli looked at Janis for a short while and Janis wondered whether he was trying to figure out how to break bad news. Then Pauli said, 'Your privileged life in Riga would have given you the opportunity to undertake fulfilling creative work and you would have found enjoyment in consuming the best of food and the highest of arts. But, there is also purpose in a life that is almost barren of creation and consumption. This purpose comes though your attitude to your existence, an existence restricted in our case by external forces.'

Pauli paused again as he could see that Janis was trying to take in what he had said. Then he recommenced. 'If there is meaning to life then there must be meaning in suffering. Suffering is part of life, as death is also part of life. Without suffering and death, life cannot be complete.

'The way in which a man accepts his fate and all the

suffering it entails, that is the way in which he takes up his cross, gives him ample opportunity, even in the most difficult of circumstances, to add a deeper meaning to his life and provides the possibility for high moral behaviour.' Pauli paused briefly, looked Janis directly in the eyes and said, 'Janis, here and now you can become a man. You can choose to make use of, or to forgo, the opportunity of attaining the moral values that this difficult situation grants you.' Janis nodded and Pauli continued, 'Someone looks down on each of us in difficult times - a friend, a father or God and he would not expect us to disappoint him. He would hope to find us suffering proudly – not miserably. Now returning to Dostoevsky, it is this attitude of which I speak that decides whether a man is worthy of his suffering or not.'

Janis began to cry and Pauli gently added, 'There is no need to be ashamed of tears, for tears bear witness that a man has the greatest of courage, the courage to suffer.' Pauli did not know that the tears were because Janis thought that he had already disappointed his father, and God for that matter, by killing Velichko.

The days shortened and the cold of another Siberian winter settled in, but Janis' spirits lifted. He became more sociable and communicative and the move towards depression was slowly reversed.

Over the next weeks and months Janis and Hilkka were constant companions. With the autumn rains giving way to snow they spent a good deal of their time talking about their past and hopes for the future. Janis found out that Hilkka was twenty-one and her mother had died when she was eight. Her older sister was a good musician and was at a music academy in Helsinki so, when they were in Finland, Hilkka often found herself cooking and cleaning and looking after her three other sisters.

Janis and Hilkka chatted surprisingly well together in Russian and as a result he pieced together her experience of the war and deportation.

Hilkka had lived in a small Finnish town by Lake Ladoga. Janis learnt that this is a freshwater lake with its southern edge starting only some forty kilometres outside the outskirts of Leningrad. Hilkka was proud to say that it is the largest lake in Europe.

Hilkka talked about her family and that her father, Pauli, used to be a cardiologist at a sanatorium on the lakeside Together with him and her sisters, she had lived in a nice wooden house painted in a burnt red colour typical of Finland. Hilkka talked about their life there and their routine. Summers were warm and there was plenty of sailing on the lake. Winters were cold and they kept active with lots of cross-country skiing. Rain, snow or shine they would go to church on a Sunday.

Hilkka proved to know quite a lot about the recent history of Finland. Janis was surprised to learn that the whole of Finland used to be part of the Russian Empire. Just as with Latvia, it was only from the time of the Russian Revolution and the Russian Civil War that Finland had become an independent nation.

Although everyone knew that their big neighbour was not happy about losing their Finnish territory, Pauli told the girls not to worry. Hilkka never reminded her father of his words, 'Russia has bigger fish to fry than starting a war with Finland.' Many other families in the village evacuated to Helsinki but Pauli said that they should keep on with their daily routine, which for her father meant visiting his wife's grave.

It was a big shock on the 31st March 1939 when Soviet troops entered their small town, shut the schools and commandeered the hospital at which Pauli worked. From then on there was no means of fleeing.

Soon, most of the remaining town folk were being piled into canvas-covered trucks and carted out of town. Pauli and his family remained behind, as suddenly there was an influx of badly wounded Red Army soldiers to the sanatorium, which was quickly turned into a field hospital. As a trained doctor and one who spoke fluent Russian, Pauli turned his hand from looking after hearts to patching, sewing and shipping off large numbers of wounded back to Leningrad.

Hilkka saw truckloads of Russian soldiers heading to the front. She wondered then why they were not wearing winter camouflage and although she knew nothing of warfare she thought that earth-brown uniforms against the snow must make them easy targets for the Finnish snipers. And so it must have proved as she saw just as many returning ambulances as she had seen trucks going west.

By January 1940 the fighting was over. Hilkka only knew that her part of Finland was back under Mother

Russia's control and it was not long before the canvas-covered trucks returned to ship any remaining Finns away from what had become a militarized zone.

Janis told Hilkka about his family and life in Latvia. They found that they both had Russian-born mothers. Hilkka's mother was born in Leningrad and had met Pauli when she had visited the sanatorium as a young woman just before the Finnish declaration of independence in 1917.

Hilkka reminded Janis of his own mother in the way that she managed to stand out from the others. Somehow, she looked smarter than the rest, her hair always seemed clean and her fingers were slender.

On one occasion, Hilkka talked about her journey to Siberia and again there were remarkable similarities with the experience of Janis. One difference was that Hilkka had not travelled in cattle trucks. The family had been put in *Stolypinka*, which were normal passenger trains that had been converted for prison use. Hilkka explained, 'All the windows were barred and the individual compartments had been removed. The walls were replaced by steel netting so that it resembled a cage. The guards could look all the away along the carriage. There were no toilets and we were only let off twice a day. At first I felt sorry for those that could not wait and had to soil their clothes but after a while I began to hate them. Jani, what do you think of that? How cruel and callous am I to hate a person just because they cannot wait to go to the toilet?' Janis liked the way that Hilkka shortened his name in the traditional Latvian way when talking to someone close. He replied, 'Yes, it is strange how we hate the people that are close to us when we should be directing our hatred elsewhere.' Janis thought of his moment of anger directed at Velichko and realised that he had struck out against the Soviet system. The foreman had just been an easy target.

Hilkka explained that her family had spent most of their time in mid-Siberia on a farm where there was a small factory. At first Pauli was put in charge of the old machinery that boiled up potatoes and created starch. The girls had to sort potatoes and pack the starch. Then they were moved and Pauli had to work on the tar facility. On hearing this, Janis was reminded of the day before his big accident that he spent chatting with Pauli.

In a quiet moment with Hilkka he told her of his worries, 'Hilkka, how can I properly look after the people whom I love?' In voicing the word 'love' he realised that he loved Hilkka. Janis looked at her, bent forward and kissed her on the lips. It was their first kiss and he thought that it was the most pleasurable thing that he had ever done.

In spending time with Hilkka, Janis also got to know Pauli and was constantly amazed that he did not curse the conditions or the system for subjecting his family to this hardship. In the quiet of the evening, Janis would chat with Pauli about nature and the wonder of the human body.

The winter came and as Janis was only able to walk short distances his fishing and hunting was very limited. He and Sonja did not starve though because Pauli kept them in hare meat and potatoes.

Release

In the spring new orders came. There were major construction works at Plahina and Janis, together with some others including Pauli, were detailed to build a large barn there. The families moved to the village and to Janis his return was welcome. He had become frustrated with the isolation of the lakes and often wondered whether he would have gone mad if he had not had the company of Hilkka. Plahina now seemed to be highly civilised.

Building the barn was incredibly physical. Janis had to be careful about his leg and now walked with a serious limp, but that did not stop him from pitching in with the men. He used his abilities with an axe to good effect and with the sawing he soon regained the muscle that had wasted away during the long recuperation. He even managed to pay off the accumulated debt of the broken equipment, lost traps and torn nets.

At the end of each day Janis went back with Pauli and spent time with Hilkka. They continued to find that they had a lot in common. Both enjoyed literature and they would sit for hours telling their best stories to each other. When they weren't telling stories Hilkka taught Janis Finnish folksongs and he accompanied her on his harmonica.

In the summer the collective farm decided to build a

cattle station so that young cows could eat the hay in the fields, which saved transporting the grass back to the farm. This meant that Janis, together with Pauli and other men and teenagers had to work away from the village and sleep in a tent at night. They had frequent visits from Hilkka who brought along water for the thirsty workers. The group was equipped with a shotgun and fishing net, and with Pauli's hunting skill, they ate well. On the odd day off they took back fish and game for the rest of the families who remained working on the collective farm.

Janis was working on the cattle station when Sonja received a notice from the Regional Commander at Igarka. It read, 'Janis Mednis, Member of the Family of an Enemy of the Revolution is herewith authorised to return to Latvia'. She was informed that all minors who had been deported in 1941 were eligible to return home. His mother also received the first letter from her daughter. In it, Ginta had written that she was now a full member of the corps de ballet and had managed to save some money, which was enclosed. Putting down the notice and the letter Sonja cried for a day.

Janis initially refused categorically to leave his mother and girlfriend, but as the days passed he began to think about returning. 'Maybe,' he thought, 'when I am back in Riga I can press for the release of my mother and find out what happened to Pappa.' As the weeks turned into a month his resolve to stay weakened. Before telling his mother of his decision to return to Riga he had one other thing to do. He went off to see Pauli and asked whether it was possible to marry his daughter.

Pauli readily agreed that he could marry Hilkka but the administration proved to be more difficult. Janis asked the Regional Officer on one of his visits to Plahina about how he could get a marriage recorded. The Regional Officer was an unsmiling man but, from what Janis understood from others, he knew him to be fair. However, what he said seemed to be completely unfair. The man's answer was short and to the point, 'All marriages are banned between Soviet citizens and foreigners.' Janis took a step back as if he had been punched in the stomach. He was about to leave when he suddenly looked up and countered with, 'Regional Officer, I would ask you to bear in mind that I don't have a passport and as an enemy of the people I have not been granted Soviet Citizenship.' For the first time in his life Janis was pleased that he was a 'non-person'.

On the next visit of the Regional Officer, Janis asked for a meeting and was told that permission had been given for him to marry. He suddenly believed in the power of prayer and Russian logic.

On the 28th of August 1948 Janis and Hilkka were married in the communal hall in Plahina. Rarely had the hall looked so pretty. In the strong sun that shone that day, and bedecked with garlands of flowers and branches from birch trees, it looked almost idyllic. Even the moskas did not bite as fiercely.

The couple followed as much as they could the Finnish traditions.

The night before the wedding Hilkka, the bride-to-be, went from house to house in Plahina with a small bag to receive wedding gifts. According to custom, the bag should have been a pillowcase but all had long since been used for other purposes. Pauli accompanied his daughter holding a makeshift parasol over her head to shelter her. It was not raining but the sheet over wooden sticks symbolised protecting the new bride. People were as generous as they could be. Sonja had made an embroidered brooch and some of the other ladies had made a lace headdress. How they managed to create lace bemused Janis.

On the day of the wedding Janis stood by Pauli waiting for his bride to enter the communal hall. It was summer and their clothes had recently been washed. Janis did not care that what they had on barely amounted to no more than rags. At that precise moment, he felt as good as if he had been wearing a top hat and tails in the Riga Dome.

Janis turned around and saw that Hilkka had arrived with her sisters and was wearing a crown on her head made of golden coloured leaves. He could not believe that he could be marrying such a beautiful woman. They stood in front of the Regional Official who, dressed in a dark jacket, looked the part, although his unsmiling face conveyed nothing of the joy that could be felt in the communal hall.

The Regional Officer pronounced them man and wife.

The wedding reception was in the communal hall and everyone in the village was invited. All brought something including rare smiles and some food even it was just potatoes. The wedding feast was laid out and in pride of place was a Siberian delicacy. The couple were honoured by being given a present of boiled horse's hooves. The jelly scraped from around the knuckles was supposed to be delicious and was also rumoured to be an aphrodisiac. Janis whispered to Hilkka, 'Luckily I don't need an aphrodisiac. Maybe I will save it until we are old.' They both laughed and let the locals eat their favourite food. Someone had brought a large jug of vodka and as glasses were in short supply, people took a swig from the communal vessel.

The bride and groom sat next to each other in designated 'seats of honour' whilst Pauli made a speech, 'Ladies and gentlemen, honoured guests, today is a day of celebration. We are here to celebrate the union of two wonderful young people and to wish them happiness in their future journey together.'

'I am a very fortunate man. I have had the love of a

wonderful wife who gave me five beautiful daughters. Although my wife and eldest daughter are not here, I can still feel their presence and I know that they are happy too for the couple.

'Last year I went on a small expedition with Janis. Adversity opens up a man's soul and I was able to see that, as Janis suffered, he is a good man; one who will be a loving husband.

'Hilkka is a special woman. Together, they will be stronger. I know that the trials and tribulations that are thrown at them, and there will be many, will be eased by being together.

'Life has delivered a different future to that which we once expected. Janis is unlikely to be the top man at the Shell company his father used to head. But maybe this is not a bad thing. Even Siberia is not as lonely a place as being the top of such an organisation. Siberia has taught me to appreciate life itself and I remain convinced that hardship is eased when we have hope and love in our hearts.

'When we have hope that daylight will replace the dark sky; when we have hope that the sun will banish the ice, and when we have hope that new life rises from the once-frozen ground, we can live life positively. But hope is not enough. Hope must be accompanied by love.

'Here are some wise words I heard a long time ago. Love is patient; love is kind. It does not envy, it does not boast, it is not proud. It does not dishonour others, it is not self-seeking, it is not easily angered, it keeps no record of wrongs. Love does not delight in evil but rejoices with the truth. It always protects, always trusts, always hopes, always perseveres.

'And now, Janis and Hilkka go forward towards a new future. There will be struggle, there will be hope and there will be love. The greatest of these is love.'

The guests were quiet for a few moments and then clapped enthusiastically. Even the Regional Officer joined in.

After the food had been quickly consumed the village orchestra assembled. It consisted of three people. One played Janis' harmonica, one played a whistle and the other a makeshift drum kit. To a unique musical treat, 'The Dance of the Crown' was performed. Hilkka's sisters, who were also the bridesmaids, blindfolded the bride and danced around her. Hilkka took off the crown and put her arm out to stop one of the dancers. Then, carefully she felt for her head and placed the crown on one of her sisters who gave an excited yell, as tradition dictated that she would be the next to marry. Hilkka took off the blindfold and hugged all her sisters.

Despite the primitive instruments the orchestra started to play a recognisable waltz. Sonja placed a round, hard-baked 'biscuit' made of oats on the bride's head, which signalled that the newlyweds would perform the first dance. This was Janis and Hilkka's first ever dance and it was not long before the biscuit fell from her head and broke into what seemed like hundreds of pieces. The bridesmaids looked at each other and burst out laughing. The biscuit should have been a china plate and such items typically smash into a few fragments. The number of pieces supposedly predicts, in Finnish custom, how many children the couple would have. However, Sonja would not hear about the waste of smashing a china plate and she made them the biscuit as a replacement. Hilkka joined in with the laughter and said to Janis, 'Don't worry, we won't have more than five children.'

March 8th 1953 – More Thoughts from Moscow

Janis realised that he had been absorbed in his Siberian experience for sometime, yet Hilkka slept on. For a while Janis turned his mind to what they would do later in the afternoon. He thought, 'When Hilkka wakes we'll walk around Moscow a little. I don't want to see Stalin's dead body but it might be interesting to see the city full of mourners.'

Lying on the single bed opposite to Hilkka, Janis began to reflect on fate and the little part that his decisions had played in his life. Fate, he concluded, had actually been kind to him.

Janis wondered what would have happened to him had he not been deported. He had found that, with a few exceptions, all his classmates had been conscripted into the army. The older boys had been forced to join the Russian Army and then, later, the younger ones had to join the German Army. He heard stories that brothers were fighting against each other in different armies. Some were released from POW camps but most did not return.

Janis thought about how lucky he had been in Siberia. He understood that his experience had been dramatically different from many others. 'I lived with caring and intelligent women and was surrounded largely by lame men in any position of authority. I could have worked at worse collective farms. I could have died in the Purga but was spared. Mamma could have died on that fateful trek had it been our turn to walk for provisions.' His thoughts turned to the last few hours with Harijs.

In his lucid moments, Harijs described the journey in which his mother perished. When the Purga blew in they were already more than half way to the collection point where they were heading for supplies. They decided to push on but they lost the path, tried to turn back and then got completely lost. They wandered around for sometime and then it seemed that their luck was in as they stumbled on a disused hut. However, when they entered the hut it was just as cold in there as outside. Harijs tried to light a fire with the firewood that had been left for future travelers, but he could not get it started as his hands were too cold to grip the matches. They could not stay and they could not move on. Harijs touched his mother's feet, which were like ice. Her last words to her son were, 'Please lay out a sheet; I'm going to die now.'

After Janis had buried his friend in a shallow grave and in a period when a large moon provided sufficient light, he went to look for the hut where Harijs' mother had laid down to die. Janis had an idea where it was and through thick snow he made his way there.

Tentatively, he pushed open the door of the hut waiting to be assaulted by the stench of decay but there all he could smell was charcoal in the old stove. By the light of the moon Janis could see Harijs' mother. She lay there frozen white and covered by a thin veneer of frost. The matches were scattered on the floor that Harijs' fingers had been too cold to properly use.

The morgue of a hut was intensely cold and with the moon partially hidden by the surrounding trees it felt eerie to Janis. Somehow, he managed to drag the stiff and heavy body outside and onto the handheld sleigh that he had brought with him. The moonlit sky and the shadows intensified the cold. As Janis pushed the sleigh over the snow the sound of it and his skis seemed to be saying her surname, 'Sneiders, Sneiders, Sneiders'. All the way back through the forest he cursed. First he cursed Siberia and then realised that it was not fair on this pristine wilderness, then he cursed Russia. Then he cursed Stalin and then he cursed himself for not being strong enough to have escaped.

Janis thought about the grave that now held Harijs and his mother. It was such a long way from their real home in Salaspils. He then recalled the short journey that he had made one day to Harijs' old home village. He had simply wanted to remember his old friend and for a change one free day decided to take a bus out of Riga.

It was autumn when Janis went to Salaspils. The gardens of the small wooden houses were full of dahlias and sunflowers scattered behind wooden fences. Apple trees strained under the weight of a bumper crop. He was just thinking that it was such a picturesque village and how happy Harijs must have been living there when, by chance, he came across a disused camp of sorts with large brick-built barracks covered by red-painted tin roofs, which were surrounded by barbed wire and watchtowers. Harijs had said nothing about a prison being there and as it was deserted he went inside the main gate to explore. As soon as he did so a chill went down Janis' spine. He felt cold to the core and wondered if the sun had disappeared but it was still bright in the sky. Janis decided that he would not go further. On returning home he asked Ginta if she knew anything about a camp at Salaspils. Ginta said that as far as she knew it was a Nazi detention centre. She had heard that many Latvians who returned from Russia in the war were sent there and she understood that it also housed Jews deported from Germany.

Janis added the fact that he was not a Jew to the lucky side of the balance sheet.

Then Janis thought how lucky he was to still have his mother whom he would soon be seeing again.

Thoughts of his mother prompted memories of Janis' childhood to come flooding back. In particular, he remembered the last summer in Riga. After the initial shock of seeing Russian tanks and soldiers on the street, life for Janis continued as it always had.

Janis' family owned a summerhouse at *Jurmala*, the seaside and he spent most of June, July and August there playing in the sand hills on the coast and swimming in the sea. His mother was there for the whole time and Janis recalled that his father had stayed for at least a month. Most of the time, Andres, his best friend, was with him as his family too had a summerhouse not far down the coast. Each morning they would meet up on bikes and plan the day, which on most occasions involved fishing and swimming.

Janis remembered that there were elections that summer. His mother and father included Ginta and himself in the political discussions that they had at the table in the garden, which they often used to eat at when they were at the summerhouse. He recalled being cautioned never to say anything about these discussions to others, especially as his father predicted that nothing good would come of the elections. As it turned out, the Latvian candidates were arrested and the only choice was for communists who duly voted for the incorporation of Latvia into the Soviet Union. Janis now smiled at the efforts that were made to delude the world that Russia had been invited into the Baltic states.

Janis' thoughts rolled on and as he shut his eyes he became more philosophical, 'Yes, fate has been kind to me. I am lucky but who is this lucky person? Who am I? How do I sum up this lucky man? I am a proud Latvian with a Russian-born mother. I am a husband. Yes, so much is clear. I am a child of an enemy of the people. No. That doesn't fit, not entirely. But I admit that I was against the people, at least the Russians. I wanted the Germans to win the war but the camp at Salaspils.... Was I right to be on their side? Am I a weed that needs to be removed from the garden?'

Janis' thoughts turned to the Stalinist propaganda that he heard so often talked of and which he had read about on the communal *Pravda* newspapers posted outside the hospital. From the front cover of the newspaper to the posters splashed around the city, it was proclaimed that a workers' revolution was building a system that would show the rest of the world the way forward. 'But,' Janis now pondered, 'did the end justify the means? Was it worth thousands of flowers being pulled up to eradicate the odd weed in order to build a better future?' He recalled the state of the collective farms and thought about the waste that he had seen. He thought about the fear and suspicion that poisoned lives and he concluded that there was no way forward when new cities were being built on the bones of forced labour.

Janis decided that there was no way of easily summing himself up. 'If there was,' he thought, 'I'd describe myself as a small boat. One that, despite its best efforts, fails to make a straight course in a heavy sea. All I am capable of is learning to ride the waves and occasionally bailing out to stay afloat.'

Janis reflected on where his thoughts had taken him and then became more unsatisfied. 'Am I a product of my background? Is that it, am I simply an output of a set of circumstances? A rudderless boat? No, surely not,' he queried.

For some reason Janis had an image of his mother sitting in the summerhouse with her embroidery and then thought, 'I am part of a tapestry that transcends me. I am part of a bigger picture that is not of my choosing. But I am in relation to the other threads in the tapestry. I haven't chosen which threads to be next to but I am always connected to them whether I like it or not. I'm not defined by the bigger picture but I am defined by my relationships.' Suddenly Janis felt more powerful than he had done for a long time. He felt that he had the freedom to choose how to respond to circumstances that were not of his making and his thoughts turned to the relationships with his wife and mother and those that he once had with his father, Andres and Harijs. He felt proud. Then he thought of the incident with Velichko and his dealings with the NKVD. Janis quickly shook himself completely awake, got up and went to the window. Outside, he could see that people were still heading into the centre of the city to pay their respects to the departed Stalin.

Janis looked over at Hilkka. Her mouth was slightly open and he could hear the breath of deep sleep. He smiled at the thought of how happy she would be at the reunion with her family.

Janis thought about the pain of separation, his own disappointing homecoming and the terrible experience he had unintentionally inflicted on Hilkka by bringing her to Riga.

Article 58

Return to Latvia

Despite having decided to return to Riga it was with reluctance that Janis gathered a few clothes into a bundle and prepared to leave.

To kisses, prolonged hugs and whispers of 'I love you,' Janis climbed aboard a small steamship, which bore him south. It was only when the whistle blew to signal its departure that he realised that he had not brought his harmonica with him. He felt that he was leaving part of himself in Siberia but hoped that he would not have to return to retrieve it.

Janis stared at the receding figures on the quayside and continued to stare beyond the wake of the steamship for some time after they had disappeared, unable to comprehend exactly what the next phase of life would entail. He felt incredibly sad about leaving his mother and wife, but was positive that returning to Riga was the right thing to do. After all, the war was over and he hung onto the idea that the deportations had happened because of the conflict.

Janis carried with him no documents except a piece of grey paper with a badly typed note from the Regional Commander at Igarka saying that he had been released of his own will from the work at the collective farm. Upon presenting his papers at Igarka he was supposed to receive a passport.

When the shipped docked at Igarka Janis found that it was a city under construction by forced labour. There was a Gulag camp not far from the city perimeter and prisoners were continually being marched through the streets. There seemed to be thousands of them and hundreds of guards with ferocious looking dogs. Boots had trodden out pathways stretching towards the prison. The paths were so narrow that it was as if the prisoners were walking on a rim and were afraid to fall off. With continual shouts from the guards of, 'One step to the left, one step to the right and we shoot,' made it clear to Janis why the paths were so. Another thing, other than the noise and bustle, which was surprising to him was the food that could be bought in the shops. But it was not the amount so much as the fact that it was all American. Janis wondered whether the Americans were supporting the deportations and forced labour at the Gulags.

After less than one day at Igarka it turned out there was no time for the formality of getting a passport. A large steamship, the Sergio Ordzanikidze, was sailing for Krasnoyarsk the next day and Janis wanted to get as far away as possible from the terrible sight of stick-thin men being marched to undertake their daily labour.

The ship was packed full of passengers. People slept in the gangways and on deck. There were free workers returning from well-paid jobs, there were criminals released from prison but there were no freed political prisoners, which was the category that Janis' father fell into.

A few days before reaching Krasnoyarsk, Janis' vessel caught up with another that had become stranded on a sandbank. This ship was the Vyacheslav Molotov and was the same vessel that Janis and Sonja had headed north on years before.

All the passengers on the stranded vessel were transferred to Janis' ship so that for its final leg it was dangerously overcrowded. People shared bunks and sat tightly packed on the crowded deck.

Janis fell into conversation with one of the newly-boarded passengers, a Russian on his way to visit his family in Krasnoyarsk. He was a free worker who enjoyed the benefits of the high wages that could be obtained by working in the Far North. Janis was surprised how chatty the man was as most of his experience with Russian men had indicated that they were taciturn when sober and crazy when drunk. The man proved to be knowledgeable about recent events and explained to Janis that the ship that ran aground was named after the current Minister of Foreign Affairs, Vyacheslav Molotov. He explained that he was the man who tried to avert war by signing the non-aggression pact of 1939. The travelling companion summed up what then happened, 'Hitler tore up the pact and rued the day that he bit the hand of the bear. Stalin kicked his arse all the way to Berlin.' The man changed subject but Janis was left wondering whether this was the same pact that allowed Russia to invade Finland and occupy the Baltic states. Later, Janis was intrigued to hear from his fellow passenger that Stalin himself had been exiled to Siberia and had passed through his next destination.

As soon as the ship reached Krasnoyarsk all papers were inspected. Janis was extremely worried, as many women ahead of him in the queue to disembark were not allowed to get off the ship. The signature on the bottom of his paper must have carried some weight as he was allowed to pass and he hurried towards the train station. There his spirits fell.

The railway station was surrounded by thousands of people all seeking to secure a prized seat on the Moscow-bound train.

Eventually, after a great deal of wandering around, Janis found a place to stay overnight. It was only the corner of a room for which he was exorbitantly charged. The next day he was advised that the only way to get on a train quickly was to buy a ticket on the black market. This cost three hundred roubles and Janis was then left with ten roubles for the remaining journey. 'At least,' he thought, 'the ticket seller asked no questions and didn't need to see any documentation.'

There were no designated seats in the passenger cars. It was up to each person to find the best place. The bunk beds were in three levels and Janis threw his very small bag of belongings onto the top one just as a large family entered the compartment. As the grandmother squeezed past Janis he noticed a small envelope drop from the top of her bag and he instinctively covered it with his shoe. The family moved on to find accommodation for them all. When they had disappeared further along the train Janis recovered the envelope and discovered that it contained money. It was not a fortune but would be enough to keep him fed on the journey. He sat for a while until the train was underway and then made his way towards where the family had gone. He found the woman who had dropped the envelope. She was with her family in the restaurant car tucking into a large supper and Janis decided that he would definitely keep the money.

The train was taking Janis home and as he got onto his bunk that night he could hear the wheels of the train call to him, 'To Latvia, to Latvia, to Latvia.'

Ten days later the train reached Moscow. Janis had spent his windfall on provisions and now had no money for a ticket back to Riga. He could not even enter the station without documents or a ticket. He spent an hour walking around the general area of Rizshkaya, the main railway station to Riga. He noted the traffic and the sooty smell of the city. He noted the crowds and the dirty exhaust of the trucks that rumbled up and down the large avenues. He noted that there were shops with food in them and queues waiting to get in. He noted much but paid little interest to it. His thoughts were focused on getting back to Riga.

Janis suddenly had what he thought was a great idea. He found out about the route of the train and then began to walk out of the city towards the first station that the Riga bound train might stop at. As he walked further out of the city he noticed how much dirtier and more neglected it became. For a brief moment, he compared the smoky, scruffy, grey city to that of the pristine wilderness of Siberia. For that brief moment he felt a pang of homesickness for the land that regularly tried to starve or freeze him to death.

It took Janis all day to walk out of the city and to the station. His feet had become hardened in Siberia to long walks but he was not used to concrete and stony paths. By the end of the walk his footwear was ragged and his feet were horribly blistered. However, he was able to forget the pain as his arrival coincided with a huge train rolling into the station. Janis could not believe his luck when it read *Na Rigu*, To Riga and, despite his tiredness, he jumped onboard. He settled behind a door in a vestibule just as the engine hooted and a massive exhalation of steam signalled the beginning of the last leg home.

When he arrived in Riga he left the train only when the cleaning lady entered the carriage. Then he ran across the tracks instead of going down the platform and into the station. Despite feeling like he had arrived as a runaway, he was pleased to have returned home.

From the railway sidings Janis could see the church spires and domes of the old city. He knew immediately that something was different and realised that the imposing spire of St Peteris Church was missing from the familiar skyline. He had never considered that the fabric of Riga might have been damaged in the war. He had only thought about the possibility of people dying.

Janis' sister, Ginta, lived in Andrejsala, which was a suburb near to the docks. With his last few kopeks Janis paid for a taxi to take him to her address. The taxi made its way through the streets of Riga that he used to know so well. On the way they went past what had once been known as *Brivibas Iela,* Freedom Street. Now he noticed that it had been renamed Lenin Street. The once-full shop windows seemed to have nothing in them and in the early evening gloom, the whole city looked darker and dirtier than he remembered.

It was dusk when he arrived at Ginta's address. This was one area of Riga that Janis had not explored and to him it looked run-down and rather dodgy. Two stray-looking dogs eyed him suspiciously from next to the communal bin. Wary cats stood guard at the door of the outside toilet. Ginta's address was in a two-storey wooden building that was covered in tarred felt, which Janis noticed to be quite common in this poor district. He looked up at the shabby house. Janis tried the door and found that it opened onto a hallway with a wooden staircase. He puckered his nose at the sharp smell of cat pee and thought, 'How strange it is that there were no cats in Siberia.' Janis went up the stairs and past a door that was ajar. Music from the room, which was lit with a faint red glow, could be heard. He reflected on how many years it had been since he had heard anything on the radio.

Janis went up another flight of creaking stairs, hoping that he had the wrong address. Then he saw his sister's name on the side of the doorframe. He knocked and his heart beat like it was trying to break out of his chest.

Ginta opened the door. It had been seven years since Janis had last seen his sister. He recognised her immediately although she was much taller and prettier than he remembered her. She looked at him initially with suspicion. Here was a man dressed in what could only be described as rags. He was young-looking but had grey hair, unkempt beard and carried a walking stick. She had not expected Janis and then suddenly she recognised her brother. They hugged each other and Ginta wept on his shoulder.

Inside Ginta's home, Janis suddenly felt incredibly dirty. He had not even considered this before but now was conscious that he could not sit on the chair offered to him. Ginta directed him to the communal washroom where there was a small sink. After a short while Ginta tapped on the door and passed through some clothes, which Janis recognised as his father's. He stayed in the washroom for a long time and tried to pick all the lice off his body. Then there was banging on the door and Janis bundled up his old clothes, took them downstairs and threw them in the dustbin outside.

When Janis got back to the room Ginta explained,

'The man banging on the door is Oswalds. He was the owner of the property before it was nationalised and has been left with two rooms downstairs. He makes an income from renting one of the rooms to anyone who will pay a small rent and keep him supplied with vodka. His daughter lives below here with her son and the old man demands payments in vodka from her for not informing on her about her night time job.' Janis must have looked a little bemused and she added, 'His daughter is a prostitute.' Janis was appalled that his sister lived above such a person.

Ginta continued with the inventory, 'The other residents in the house are a Jewish student by the name of Binjamin Elon and a Russian couple.'

That night, brother and sister talked together into the early hours. Eventually, Janis approached the topic that had been hanging in the air for some time. Hesitantly he asked. 'Have you heard anything of father?' The answer shocked him. With tears welling up, Ginta quietly said, 'I made enquiries and father was reported as having died of pneumonia in Vjatlag.' To Janis this was inconceivable. After a short silence he said, 'But father walked around in winter without a scarf. Remember how he often went swimming in the River Daugava right up to when it froze over? Pneumonia, no!' Janis could not believe that, 'But he never had even a cold before.'

Article 58

Life in Riga

On the first full day in Riga Janis reported to the Militia as he had been instructed to do. He had assumed that the process would be to register for a passport and then, as a legal inhabitant, he would be able to find a job. Janis planned that after obtaining employment he would bring back his wife and press for the release of his mother. The first question from the official who took his paper was, 'How much did you pay for this?' It was at this precise moment that Janis realised that his status had not changed. He was still an enemy of the people and felt that he had been physically thumped in the stomach. After his details had been logged and with a heavy sinking feeling he made his way back to Ginta's *dzīvoklis*, flat.

Ginta's home could not really be called a flat and certainly not an apartment. It was a small attic with a sloping ceiling that consisted of a tiny sitting room with a thin couch and a bedroom, which was almost entirely taken up with a single iron bedstead and a wardrobe. Ginta explained that in the summer it was hot and in the winter it was freezing. Janis assured his sister that he would not be troubled with the cold. The toilet was a foul-smelling communal one outside and the kitchen, which was also communal, consisted of three old oil-fired cookers. There was a smell of petroleum indicating that lighting the stoves involved taking your life into your hands. Greasy plates piled up in the sink. It could not have been more of a contrast to the apartment that they once had as their home in Alberts Street.

Janis recognised the couch and the few ornaments on a small table. Ginta explained that she had been able to gather up some possessions before their apartment had been turned over for communal use. When he picked up the silver photograph frame, which contained a picture of his mother and father on their wedding day, Janis felt his tears welling up. His parents looked so young. His father was especially handsome in his Latvian Rifleman's uniform and those polished boots that he had seen disappearing into the distance so many years ago. It suddenly struck him that he had not cried much during all the long hard years in Siberia. 'If I start now,' he thought, 'I might not stop.'

Although there was little space, Ginta insisted that her brother stay with her rather than look for somewhere else until Hilkka's arrival. The couch proved to be as comfortable as a feather mattress to Janis.

The next day, Janis went to look at his old family residence. It was only seven years since he had lived there but when he turned into Alberts Street, it looked like a century had passed. Some of the plaster on the art nouveau facades had fallen off and there were broken windows, which looked like no one was going to mend quickly. From inside some of the apartments he could smell food being fried and the sound of screaming children. The communal door of the block in which Janis used to live was open and he went in and up the cat pee-smelling stairs to his family's old apartment. The door was shut but opposite he could see into the now shabby apartment that was once owned by their good friends, the Siegalmans. In the hall were about eight pairs of boots and a line of poor-looking dirty coats. Clearly there were a number of families now living here. A child of about ten with a grubby face came into the hall, saw Janis, and quickly disappeared. Janis made his exit.

Janis and Ginta talked that evening and Janis shared some of the stories that involved his mother and her cooking, fishing and embroidery prowess. He failed to tell her how close she had come to dying on more than one occasion and how fragile her clutch on life really was in Siberia. After all winter was fast approaching and he did not want to worry his sister.

Janis asked, 'Ginta, how did you manage to keep safe and not be deported?' Ginta replied, 'You remember that on that fateful evening in June 1941 I was staying with the Plavnieks at their summerhouse. The Plavnieks simply adopted me into their family and I stayed with them for a while. Dr. Plavnieks wasn't under suspicion and then soon after Pappa, Mamma and you were taken away the war started. It looks like the Soviet leadership had other worries for a while, which were bigger than making sure that all the Mednis' were sent to Siberia.'

Janis thought of his time as a patient in the hospital and said, 'I remember Dr. Plavnieks, is he still the Director?' Ginta responded, 'No. He was arrested as a saboteur when the X-ray machine at the hospital broke down. Of course it was simply an excuse to replace him. He wasn't deported but he was reduced to working as a general doctor. The Plavniek family no longer live in the big apartment on Vilandes but I'm friends still with Mara. She is in the corps de ballet with me.' Janis remembered the Plavnieks' tall and skinny daughter.

Having graduated from the Ballet School, Ginta now was a professional dancer and worked at the Opera House. She was up early and often out until late when there was a performance. Janis did not like the idea of his sister coming home late to their neighbourhood. He had decided that it was not only dodgy, it was also a positively dangerous area. Oswalds' daughter attracted an irregular flow of visitors from the docks and from the rooms below Janis heard the sounds of crashing, outbursts of cursing and sobbing. When Janis offered to escort his sister back from the Opera House after the performance she refused and said that she was stronger than she looked.

Several weeks passed without any contact from the Militia.

In the absence of any other work to do, Janis went every morning to the River Daugava where he and his father used to swim. There was a small sandy beach there. Bright rays of a low sun would glint off the golden tower of the Russian Orthodox Church. It was a scene that was very familiar except that the nearby bridge was a tangled mess. Janis was unsure whether the retreating Russian Army or the retreating German Army had destroyed it to prevent easy access to the city by the respective invaders.

After a long wait Janis finally received a summons to

the Militia station and this was the start of many visits. He had to go day after day and it was always the same process. Each time he was interrogated, the questions were always repeated, 'Who are you working for? How did you come to be a spy? Who recruited you?' Then he had to sign a record of the interview. After waiting an hour or two he would be called in to see another interrogator and the scene was replayed. Eventually and after many visits to the Militia a personal code was issued together with the necessary papers. These restricted Janis' movements so that he could not leave Riga.

After Janis had received his personal code the next step was to register his address. However, he found that only employed people could register. He smiled at this news because he knew that only people who had a registered address could be employed! Here was more of the Russian logic that his mother said that he would learn about.

Janis decided to find out whether any of his old school friends were still in Riga and if they could help him get a job. One Sunday, he set out on the number eleven tram to Mezaparks to find Andres who once was his best friend and used to live there. The tram jolted and clattered its way to the Lycee Francais, his old school, and then on past a large cemetery.

Janis had made the journey many times before to the cemetery. Together with his mother he used to visit the graves of his grandparents. They were buried in a small plot deep into the wooded cemetery. Having not travelled this route for some time, Janis' thoughts returned to the day of his Grandmother's funeral. It was the first funeral that he had attended and he was rather shocked when, at the graveside, the coffin lid was lifted to reveal the waxy face of the deceased.

Janis remembered how all the little plots were well-tended and how pleasant it was to sit there in the summer amongst the simple headstones and dappled shade from the big pine trees. Now, looking into the cemetery from the window of the tram it looked rather overgrown. Then he realised that he needed to mark the death of his father somewhere and decided to talk to Ginta about the possibility of having some sort of commemorative plaque put alongside the headstones of his grandparents.

The tram trundled onto the terminus at Mezaparks where the driver moved to the opposite end of the car after reversing the seatbacks so that the tram did not need to turn around.

Just as Janis had done many times before, he made his way into the leafy suburb of Mezaparks and towards the house of Andres. It was clear that all the big houses and villas that were there had been nationalised. Large amounts of washing now hung from windows and communal washing lines. Janis then felt rather foolish and asked himself, 'Why didn't I think that, just like my family, Andres would also have been deported or at least evicted?' Nevertheless, he made his way towards his friend's old place and, with every house he passed, became a little more depressed. The villas looked unkempt and the gardens were overgrown. Every house used to have a lovely plot for vegetables but now weeds had taken hold.

Janis easily found Andres' house, opened the gate, walked up the path and rang the bell without any hope that his friend would still be there. Andres opened the door and immediately recognised Janis. Both were speechless and then they hugged.

Andres invited Janis in and apologised that he now only had a few rooms that he could call his own. Janis vividly remembered Andres' parents but now there was no sign of them.

There was a silence whilst Andres boiled water for tea. Janis was unsure where to start but broke the silence with a question, 'Did you ever have to leave Riga?' There was a long pause. Janis wondered if his friend was now pondering on how much he could say.

After handing the tea to Janis, Andres told what had happened to him and his family. It was a brief summary; just the facts and Janis knew then that his best friend was being cagey. He thought, 'Andres thinks that I could be working with the NKVD.' Although the story was brief, it was clear to Janis that they had both experienced something similar.

Andres explained, 'Mother and I were taken by freight car to Novosibirsk where the train divided. Our car went to Tomsk and there we were taken by barge to Parabela where we had to work on a collective farm for about a year and a half. At first I had pleurisy and could not work but later I undertook a range of duties including being a field hand. In the autumn I had to pick berries on Death Island. In 1943 I got a job as a surveyor's helper to a man called Mikhail Vasilyevich Chernov. May the sand rest lightly on him.'

Andres provided other facts and Janis realised that he was being given the 'official' version of his deportation; the sort of thing that he would, by now, have told the authorities plenty of times.

Janis asked, 'What about your mother? Is she still in Siberia?' Andres did not reply immediately and then said, 'Mother worked as a log lifter at the mouth of the River Keta. One day she fell in and had to return home to change her clothes. She froze to death on the way to the house.' Nothing more was added and Janis did not press for more details or ask about Andres' father.

Janis briefly told his story. In talking about this he already felt that he was looking in at someone else's life. Did he really experience this?

Janis asked Andres about whether he had managed

to find a job. Andres told him that he had found obtaining work to be difficult but had managed to commence employment working in the city's sewers. Janis tried to make a joke about this being the bottom of the pile but neither laughed. Andres said that he would see if there were any other positions available but from his tone it was clear that he would not be contacting Janis again.

The meeting ended with a rather formal handshake. The initial pleasure of friends reunited had given way to a cool atmosphere. On the way back, Janis reflected on the experience and understood just how corrosive suspicion is.

When Janis returned to his sister's apartment Ginta was already home and had good news for him. As soon as he entered the room she said, 'Mara had a word with her father and he has spoken to the Head of Administration at the hospital. They need general hands and she has agreed to take you on. It will be simple duties and cleaning but it is something.' To Janis it felt like he was given his first post as a practising doctor.

Article 58

Article 58

Introduction to the Urki

Janis started his work as a general hand in the hospital on 1st November 1948. His induction was simple; he was provided a brown overall, handed a bucket and mop, some caustic soda and told to wash the corridor and floor of Ward Ten.

The hospital had changed since Janis had been a patient there nearly ten years previously. He noticed that it was grubbier and more people were squashed on the wards. There seemed to be less equipment around although signs showed that the x-ray machine, which he had been fascinated by as a teenager, was still there.

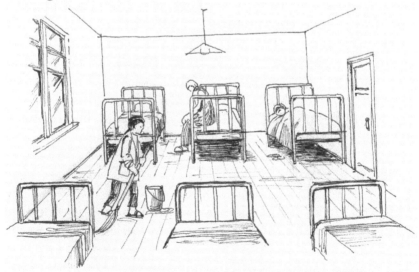

Janis immediately recognised Ward Ten. The layout had changed but he was transported back to the time when he was a patient there and chatting to the Chess Champion. He could almost hear the animated discussion and the friendly cajoling of the nurses for people to eat the rather tasty hospital food or take their medicine. No one chatted now. The ward was in silence and a few very grumpy-looking nurses stood over a desk completing paperwork. Janis got on with his work without comment from anyone and he thought, 'It looks like I have found a way of becoming invisible.'

The first day's work consisted of washing floors and taking the bedpans to the disposal area in the basement. At the end of the day, he made his way to the changing room for the general hands. It too was in the basement and a single electric bulb cast a dull light over a few rickety lockers from which the keys had long since disappeared. There he met two of his work colleagues. The introductions were brief but as the days passed and with time to talk at the end of the shifts the conversations grew longer and friendlier. Whenever they were alone together in the changing room they made a point of addressing each other as *tovarishch*, comrade, an endearment that was denied them in Siberia. There they were, at best, called *grazhdanin*, citizen.

Little by little Janis pieced together how the hospital operated and the lives of his fellow workers.

Janis soon found that Russians managed the hospital and that the doctors and nurses were mainly Latvians although they had to speak Russian. The Latvian language was not allowed to be used on the wards. There was a distinct pecking order and this was vividly manifested in the toilet facilities. The senior administration enjoyed the benefits of good plumbing on the fifth floor with separate toilets. The doctors had their own area but the toilets were Russian style allowing no seclusion to sit and ponder on the state of the world. The nurses were less well off. Then there was the toilet that the porters and general hands had to use. These were foul-smelling holes over which you had to squat.

With the job of general hand came the cloak of invisibility and when Janis was head-down sweeping and mopping he was amazed at what he could overhear and find out. He particularly enjoyed cleaning around the stores area of an evening once the managers and senior staff had gone home. He noticed how some of the nurses and doctors would furtively come there around seven and disappear into a store. Then the heavy door would be locked. For a while Janis would not be able to hear anything but then voices would be raised and there was laughter. On one occasion singing could be heard. Then, an hour later, the door would be unlocked and the inhabitants would spill out trying to hide a severe level of intoxication. The door of the store was always locked. It was obvious what was in there but it was some time later that he was officially informed that this was where the neat alcohol was kept. 'With some juices added it must make a pleasant cocktail,' thought Janis.

Over time he got to know five general hands. All had, at some time, been deportees. Most had similar tales to Janis to tell of deprivation, starvation, loss of parents, cruelty, the odd moments of joy and the sublime beauty of Siberia, but a man called Kaspars stood out. He had been sent as a convict to Siberia. That meant that he had been the subject of the Soviet criminal system and had been transported with criminals and political prisoners to the Gulags in Siberia.

Kaspars looked implacably angry and initially Janis was afraid of offending him lest it resulted in a physical eruption. But, as time went on, he realised that Kaspars' demeanor was simply an adopted survival strategy, which hid a sensitive personality. Over time, Janis appreciated that Kaspars had learnt to defend himself in an environment where any triviality could cost you your life. He came to understand that you had to be on guard, ready to take instant action and never give an inch. You had to be afraid of no one. Indeed you had to make others fearful of you.

Kaspars used to work for the Latvian Gas Company and as part of his job he had to visit many houses to deal with supply issues. His employment ceased after he was accused and convicted of stealing a silver urn from a Russian Officer's house. The sentence was ten years imprisonment, which meant being shipped off to Siberia. When the urn was later found in the house of a well-known thief the sentence was revoked. However, it still took two years for the release to come through. No apology was given and Kaspars was still regarded as a suspicious person.

In the workers' changing area they used to have

conversations about the war. All Janis' colleagues were clear that Stalin had played a vital role in winning the war. If anyone had a different opinion they kept it to themselves. About Stalin, you could only say great things or nothing at all. Even down in the basement it was clear that walls have ears.

If talking about Stalin was off limits, Kaspars openly and often talked about his time in the Soviet prison system and the Gulag. In particular he talked about the criminals whose company he had had to endure for over two years.

On the first occasion that Kaspars opened up, he talked about the living conditions in *Krasnaya Presna*, one of the prisons in Moscow through which he passed on his way to the Gulag. Kaspars said, 'If you stood at the window you could just see the Kremlin with its red star. It was about +30 degrees outside and in the cell but it seemed twice that. Everyone stripped off and sweated. You can't imagine the sharp smell of twenty unwashed male bodies in that hot and cramped space. One hour spent there seemed to be like a day. Sleeping was the worst part. You were afraid of being attacked and could not go to sleep. Even if you wanted to it was almost impossible. It was stiflingly hot and the electric lights were kept on all the time. You coudn't roll onto your side as your hands needed to be seen by the guards at all times. If they couldn't see your hands the guards would come into the cell and rudely awaken you. Then from seven in the morning to eleven at night you couldn't lie down and had stand or sit upright.'

On another occasion, Kaspars explained, 'The

criminal world has its own hierarchy and at the top are the *urki,* professional criminals. They even have their own language. For objects of particular interest such as money, prostitutes and extortion there are literally hundreds of words. They even have a word for a thief who steals from a church – *Klyukvennik.* This is *blatnoe slovo,* thieves' talk.'

Kaspars painted what was for Janis a horrendous picture, 'The highest-ranking criminals not only talk differently, they look and walk differently. They have a bizarre fashion sense and often wear crucifixes adorned with naked ladies. You couldn't imagine such a thing. They walk by taking small steps with their legs apart.' An image of a baboon came to Janis. Kaspars continued, 'Tattoos tell their own story. There are tattoos for homosexuals, rapists and murderers and they provide endless amusement for the wearers. Those that show a stoker hurling coal into the backside of Lenin or Stalin seem to create the best laughs.'

Kaspars explained that card-playing rituals were one part of the terror that the criminals exerted over the political prisoners. When playing each other, they bet bread, money and clothes. When they lost theirs, they bet the clothes of the political prisoners. Few 'politicos' risked the consequences of not giving up their possessions to a lost bet.

Kaspars often recounted scenes that he had witnessed. In one, a thief had staked the good suit of a newly-arrived political prisoner. When he lost the bet he was disappointed to find that the political prisoner had been moved and he was unable to extract the suit to pay off his debt. The Council of Senior Urki met to hand out the punishment. The plaintiff asked that all fingers be cut off his opponent's left hand for failing to honour the bet. The defendant argued for two and in the end they settled for cutting off three fingers.

Another tale involved a criminal losing at cards and then accusing the other of cheating. His last words to the alleged cheat were, 'I am the hunter and you are the hare.' Soon after, the man obtained an axe and struck the cheat over the head with the butt then split his head open with the blade. The hunter had been sentenced to twenty years in prison. He was given another ten and his file grew by a page.

Janis thought that the urki must be the worst part of prison life, then one day Kaspars talked about the *starosta*, the 'trustees' who were put in charge of a hut full of other prisoners. Kaspars began, 'The starosta in charge of our hut welcomed us with a speech in which he gave us his word that he personally would hang us from the beam, which he pointed to, if he found that people had smuggled in money or other valuables and had not declared them to him. He said that he had been authorised to do this. His beatings of inmates for failing to turn lights out on the appointed minute or for talking at night were never challenged.

'Most of the political prisoners are soon degraded but not the starosta. On the contrary they were promoted and some never before felt so powerful.'

Sometimes Kaspars would assume an ironic tone and

once tried to sell the benefits of the Gulag, 'Gentlemen, I recommend a stay in one of the country's famous retreats. You will learn much and develop a curiosity and capacities that you never realised you possessed.'

'You will became a detached observer and a curious one at that. You will ask yourself, for example, is this what it feels like to march at my own funeral, or will I freeze if I am made to stand outside naked in the chill of late autumn?

'Curiosity will turn into surprise. Once you were a light sleeper and would wake with the faintest noise. Now, you will surprise yourself by sleeping like a baby even though you are inches way from the loudest snorer you have ever heard and your arm is resting on the crook of your almost dislocated arm. Or you will be surprised how long you can live without changing your shirt. Then you will lose your curiosity and when nothing surprises you will be simply part of an enormous mass of people. After that, your existence descends to the level of animal life.'

Janis could not help contrasting Kaspars' experience with that of Pauli's expressed views. He remembered clearly what Pauli had said to him whilst he was recuperating in his house, 'Man is an irreducible mystery. Everything can be taken from a man but one thing; the last of the human freedoms - to choose one's attitude in any given set of circumstances, to choose one's way.' Pauli had clearly expressed his belief to Janis that even though conditions such as lack of sleep, insufficient food and even brute force suggest that we are bound to react in certain ways, in the final analysis it is clear that the sort of person that we become is the result of some inner decision and not the result of external influences alone. Janis wanted to believe this too but Kaspars' stories of the urki and starosta dominating everyone were so overwhelming that he thought that he would not have been strong enough to choose his own way.

Kaspars used to pull Janis' leg and once said, 'You wouldn't last five minutes in the Gulag. The iron broom of the Soviet system sweeps only rubbish into its camps. You are too soft. The only way to survive is to quickly harden up, to lie, cheat and sleep easy at night knowing that you've got one rung up on the ladder at the expense of your cellmate. There is no room for self-sacrifice. You can only survive when you have been degraded enough to show no compassion.

'Everything that is not connected with the immediate task of keeping yourself alive has to lose its value. You need to become insensitive and focus on one task; that of preserving your own life.

'Everything that you held dear has to drop from you and culture or refinement is ground into the dust. If you cannot communicate with the fist or a stick you are lost. No, Janis, you would be dead inside of a fortnight.'

In his defence Janis wanted to say, 'But Kaspars, I have killed a man,' but this only added to his sense of weakness.

It was clear that Kaspars had been in great fear of the criminals in the camp and in repeating some of the scenes, Janis assumed that this was an attempt to lessen the horror. It had the reverse effect on Janis who could hardly bear to listen to some of the recollections. It was clear that the criminals were the allies of the camp administration and were used to break the other inmates, especially those classified as enemies of the people.

The end result of all these tales was to fill Janis with dread that he should ever be taken into prison.

Article 58

The Second Wave

Despite having found a job, Janis was continually summoned to the Militia. Although he constantly referred to the order that had been given to release all those deported as minors, they insisted that he had run away from Siberia. He was surprised how much time was wasted on him and eventually came to the conclusion that there must be more dangerous alternatives that the Militia chose not to pursue. After all, there were still freedom fighters roaming around the Latvian forest and they had guns. 'Dealing with me is much safer,' he thought.

Janis felt a stranger and one with a precarious foothold in his own country. Despite this, he wrote to Hilkka. He was not sure of whether the letter would ever reach her, but hoped that with the power of love over hatred and cruelty it would find its way to her.

Dearest Hilkka,

I miss you deeply. Each day I remember our wedding and the happy times that we had together. Every night I go to sleep with your hand in mine and think of the days that we spent talking and singing.

Of course I am pleased to be back in Riga and you cannot imagine my joy at seeing Ginta once again but, without you, my happiness can never be complete.

Please do let me know soon that you have been authorised as my wife to come to Riga. I look forward to receiving some letter from you.

Ginta has said that when you arrive we can stay with her. There is not much room and we will have to make do with sleeping on a settee but once you are here we can start to look for our own flat.

I have started to work at the hospital. I always wanted to be in medicine so my wish has come true!

Please do pass on my dearest wishes to your father and sisters. I am writing to my mother separately but, if you do see her, please give her a big hug from me.

Yours lovingly

Janis did not want to write too much more as he suspected that censors would be monitoring his communications.

No reply came and the year moved on, then it tipped into 1949. Janis concluded that love had been beaten in the battle and had its heart speared by the dark forces that prevailed.

The work at the hospital involved long hours but took up little mental capacity. In the evenings and other free time Janis devoured any book that he could get hold of and at work he pondered on the stories that he had read. Ginta had taken what books she could from their family apartment and had acquired a few more secretively from friends at the ballet. Janis read them all and when he had finished them he reread them, often late into the night. He particularly enjoyed historical works and he found out as much as he could about the life of political prisoners in exile in tsarist times. He was surprised to learn that deportations were pretty common practice and that the political prisoners were described as friends of the people. 'How different from today. Now they are conveniently labeled as enemies of the people to ensure that no one feels sympathy towards them,' Janis mused.

Through his sister, Janis got hold of a book called 'Siberian Exile'. He kept this well hidden in their room, as the title itself would have created suspicion in those whose job it was to control what people were reading. In this, Janis read about the life of an exile at the beginning of the twentieth century. He was surprised to learn that at the time the government paid a certain amount to political deportees. It was not a great deal but enough so that they did not need to work. Some of them went fishing and hunting but this was for sport more than survival. Janis also knew that many fell into alcoholism. Alcohol had always been incredibly cheap and Janis wondered whether this was simply a way of subduing workers' unrest and degrading political prisoners.

On the 24th March 1949, Janis went to Kaspars' birthday party. Kaspars lived in Pardaugava, which meant literally on the other side of the river. Quite by chance Janis met a man there, Edvins Spilve, who had been in the Gulag at Vjatlag and asked, 'Did you know my father, Reinis Mednis?' Spilve replied, 'Yes.' After a lengthy pause and, just as Janis thought that he was not going to be provided any further detail, he added, 'I've signed a paper forbidding me to reveal anything,' but Janis wondered what he wanted to hide. He had survived somehow when most of the others had died in the first winter.

What Spilve did say to Janis was revealing, 'If only one man survives in ten thousand you can imagine the conditions.' Then Janis asked another question, 'Were you in the Latvian Riflemen?' Splive shook his head. Janis looked down at the man's boots, which were of the sort issued to officers in the Latvian Riflemen and thought of his father heading off on the morning of their deportation into the early morning sun in his polished boots.

It was only much later that Janis heard that at Vjatlag some of the prisoners who refused to sign a statement that they were spies were doused in water and sent out in freezing winter conditions.

It was towards midnight when Janis returned home. Passing Uzvaras Laukums, which was now dedicated to the Soviet victory in winning the Second World War, he saw a great congregation of canvas-covered trucks and men in uniform. With a dreadful feeling of foreboding he hurried back to his sister's attic and ushered her out into the yard, where they hid amongst the kindling wood in a shed.

It was in the early hours when a truck rumbled over the cobbles and stopped in front of the block where they lived. Soldiers and officials entered the building and Janis relived the night when he and his parents were first taken from their apartment. Something very similar was happening again. After a while, they saw the soldiers bring out the Jewish student, Binjamin, and he was loaded onto the truck together with a small case.

Janis and his sister did not return to the attic for the next few days. News slowly crept in from the countryside. From there, thousands of farmers had forcibly been deported.

Janis escaped the first wave of deportations that spring and returned to his work. However, he expected to be arrested at any time. On each occasion that he left home or the hospital he expected to be greeted by a barrel of a rifle. He found it difficult to sleep at night. Every creak and crack made him sit bolt upright. He managed to have a laugh about this with Ginta by telling her of the joke that was going around. It involved a couple who were also worried about the knock on the door in the middle of the night. Then one night it came. The couple were mightily relieved to find that it was their neighbour telling them that the apartment block was on fire!

Janis talked to his remaining colleagues at work at the beginning of one of their shifts. Kaspars had disappeared and so had two other fellow workers. Janis asked, 'Don't you think that it is strange that our deported colleagues all had surnames that began with the first five letters of the Russian alphabet? Do you think that the NKVD are arresting people in alphabetical order?' The men laughed but not too hard for it just struck them that this could be true.

The rest of Janis' workmates were in a similar

position to him in that they constantly waited for their deportation orders. They discussed the possibility of fleeing to the forest where there were still freedom fighters waiting for the British Tommies to help them. They decided though that they would never come out alive. It was clear that Russia was here to stay and no one was coming to their aid. They talked about the possibility of getting to Sweden but they did not have access to a boat.

Janis wondered whether he had ever thought of escape before. He could easily have slipped into the crowd that surrounded the train on that first day of his exile. But he reminded himself that he was a boy of fifteen then and had just been separated from his father whom he expected to be reunited with later in the trip.

Weeks turned into months and then a knock on the door came late one evening. Janis rose from his chair and, in a manner that resembled a man resigned to his fate, he opened the door. There he was greeted by the smile of his wife, Hilkka.

Hilkka's Arrival

Janis hugged Hilkka and only after the salty tears had almost dried on his cheeks did he usher her inside. Ginta was in the attic and had seen the reunion. Now Janis made the introduction. Ginta's Russian was heavily accented and so too was Hilkka's but they were able to communicate. Ginta went to the bedroom and offered some clothes for Hilkka to change into.

Just like Janis had done when he arrived from Siberia, Hilkka spent a long time in the communal washroom and when she came out she was wearing a dress that he recognised as one of his mother's favourites. He was surprised just how well it fitted around her slim waist. Ginta made an excuse that she needed to pick something up from work and left the couple despite it being late into the evening.

Hilkka had only a very small bag with her and out of this she took Janis' harmonica. Janis could not have been given a more special present. It came with a whole set of memories of singing and talking with Hilkka.

Hilkka informed Janis that his mother had found a job as a nurse's aid in Igarka. Janis was relieved that she was safe and well. For a while there was no talking, the couple simply held hands. Then Janis lent forward and kissed Hilkka.

After a short while, Janis took Hilkka's hand and guided her into Ginta's bedroom. He unbuttoned her dress and felt the skin of her neck, arms and shoulders. He could not believe how smooth and warm she was. Desire built and was quickly dissipated. Janis knew that he had much to learn about lovemaking.

Squashed next to Hilkka on the thin single bed, Janis said, 'You've made me the happiest man in Riga. Tomorrow we can start to look for our own place.'

Ginta did not come back that night and in the morning the couple woke in each other's arms.

Janis realised that he could not start to look for a place straight away. Firstly, he had to register Hilkka and was not looking forward to the process. Secondly, he had to go to work. He left Hilkka sitting in her pretty dress and his last words before he departed were, 'Ginta should be back this afternoon, but please don't go wandering around the neighbourhood. It is not safe. Now, bye my love and I will get back as soon as I can this evening.' On his way to work, Janis regretted saying that to Hilkka. He thought that he might be being over-protective and had essentially imprisoned her in a poky attic. However, he resolved not to let those thoughts spoil his day. He was reunited with his beautiful wife.

Two days after her arrival in Riga, Janis accompanied Hilkka to the Militia and asked for the necessary registration documents. They were told to sit and someone would attend to them. They sat and sat. The morning turned into afternoon and eventually they were escorted to a room where a man in a grey jacket sat with his chest puffed up behind a desk full of papers. Somehow the man reminded Janis of a big grey coloured crow of the type that he used to see in Siberia.

'Documents,' the crow demanded. Janis handed over his papers and Hilkka passed over the letter from the Regional Commander in Igarka stating that she was released from the Register of Deported People and was free to travel to join her husband in Riga. Janis suddenly wondered whether Hilkka had been lucky enough never to have been registered in the first place. The Finns were simply gathered up and no documentation existed. 'Has our future rested on the Commander wanting an easy life and a neat list – no one unaccounted for?' Janis mused.

The crow brought Janis back to the moment by asking, 'How much did you pay for this?' The question was no easier to deal with despite its familiarity. More questions were asked and at the end, the crow slammed his claw on the table and shouted, 'Finns, Jews, Gypsies, you are all the same. Get out, you are persona non grata.'

The couple left the building both trying to stem the flow of tears. After about twenty minutes of simply walking hand in hand, Janis said, 'Look, all it means is that finding work will be difficult but I have a job and there is Ginta too who can help out. Let's focus on finding a new flat for us.' His reassuring words seemed to cheer up Hilkka but he wondered whether it would be possible to find a new home without both of them having proper papers.

Over the next four days Hilkka had to spend time alone in Ginta's attic as both Janis and his sister were at work. Janis did not like leaving Hilkka all day for there was nothing that she could read. Hilkka had learnt to speak Russian but could not read it and the only books in Ginta's room were either in Latvian or Russian.

One day and after a particularly bad night perched on the edge of the couch, Janis asked Ginta how he could start a search for a new flat. 'Honestly Jani, I don't think that you will be able to find another place to stay. If people take in persona non grata they run the risk of being denounced.' He suddenly realised that he had put his sister at risk and his look of concern prompted her to say, 'Don't worry about me.'

A little later on Ginta said, 'Jani, you can both stay here but I know that you need your own room. If you do need to move out you could ask Oswalds downstairs if he will rent his spare room to you. At least it has a proper bed in it. His son has recently moved out – probably gone to prison. I don't like the thought of you being near the drunkard but if you give him enough vodka he won't say anything to the authorities.' Janis immediately thought about Velichko who was the last drunk he lived nearby to. He thanked his sister and said, 'Let's think on that.'

Janis did think on it and came to the conclusion that renting Oswalds' spare room might be their only option. A few days later Ginta found Oswalds in a reasonable state of sobriety and negotiated the price for the room and the daily quota of vodka.

Article 58

Before Janis let Hilkka see the room, which comprised an iron bedstead with a horribly stained mattress, wardrobe, small table and two chairs, he swept and washed it as much as he could. It took some time with the window open to hide the smell of stale tobacco from the former occupant. Eventually he allowed Hilkka to see the room. 'I know it's not a dream home but with some feminine touches it will be fine.' Janis looked up at the unshaded light bulb that hung down from the ceiling illuminating their poverty. Then he looked at the table with its ring marks and the scuffed chairs. One had a spring that was about to force its way through the thin fabric. 'What do you think?' Hilkka, as ever, gave a positive response, 'At least there are no bed bugs.' Janis was not entirely sure about that.

With a strong sense that he was letting his wife down, the couple moved into Oswalds' spare room. He remembered how he had described to Hilkka how beautiful Riga was. Now, he presented her with a dingy room, in a rundown house, in a squalid district with a drunkard for a landlord and a prostitute as a neighbour.

Life quickly settled into a routine. Janis went to work and Hilkka went shopping at the central market. This was her big treat for the day and she would recall to Janis what she had seen there. Stalls of fruit and vegetables were still seen as wondrous and when strawberries started to appear they were the main topic of conversation. Hilkka spent time cleaning the cooker in the kitchen that was allocated for Oswalds' use and she started to cook rather tasty meals for Janis.

Occasionally, Janis and Hilkka would hear Oswalds shuffling about but rarely caught sight of him. Oswalds' life was largely nocturnal and his night time activity involved banging on the wall if he ever heard Janis and Hilkka making love. Due to this the couple learnt to be quiet and stifle sounds. In the mornings, evidence of his night time activity was left in the form of dirty pans and plates in the sink.

Janis used to rush back from work as quickly as he could. He was conscious that Hilkka had very little to do and with no family around and no one who spoke Finnish there was a danger of her becoming lonely. However, whenever he got back to the room, he was always met with a smile and something to eat. Most evenings they would talk about the day and its interesting points such as the seasonal produce that appeared at the central market. Hilkka was always amused that the varieties of potatoes had girls' names and she especially liked the type that was called Andretta. It was as domestic a bliss as Hilkka could summon.

A Trip to the Seaside

After a month of living in Oswalds' spare room, Janis felt that Hilkka needed to have a change of scene and he suggested that when he next had some time off he would take her to see his family's old summerhouse in Jurmala.

It was a fine summer's day when Janis and Hilkka set off on the short journey to Jurmala. Wisps of cloud were in a blue sky and, whilst waiting for the train to the coast, Janis had the feeling that he really could be off on his summer holidays.

The steam train chugged quickly out of Riga and across the fields towards Jurmala. Just before it arrived at the coast, it crossed the Lielupe River and Janis looked across to the reed-fringed edges. He told Hilkka how he had cycled once to this area with Andres to go fishing and had taken home enough to feed both families. Hilkka playfully feigned ignorance and said, 'So, fishing is a sport as well.' Both remembered the terrible conditions on the ice in the Far North.

Janis explained to Hilkka that Jurmula was a coastal strip along Riga Bay and that they would be getting off at a stop called Dzintari. When they arrived there, Janis was surprised that the village had little changed. The houses were in remarkably good order and there were neat gardens and vegetable patches.

As they walked together toward the promenade they came across many Russian Officers strolling along with their families. It soon became apparent that Jurmala had become a playground for senior Russian military officers. 'A place by the sea; their just reward for winning the war.' Janis remarked.

The couple made their way onto the edge of the white sandy beach and for the first time since he had arrived back in Riga, Janis felt at home. The lapping sea, the sand dunes and the fir trees by the Baltic coast were just as he remembered the scene. He breathed deeply and together with Hilkka started to walk towards his old summerhouse. After a few steps on the soft sand, Janis realised that a great deal had changed since he had last been here. Now his left leg made him unsteady and he had to take Ginta's arm to keep himself from toppling over on the sand.

The family's old summerhouse was not right on the coastline and they had to head into the fir trees that nudged up to the sandy edge. After a few minutes Janis stood in front of a wooden house with stained glass in the windows and a lovely veranda. He expected his mother to come out any second and call Andres and himself in for refreshments. 'It is delightful,' said Hilkka. 'It is,' agreed Janis and added, 'I used to climb the cherry tree over there.' In pointing to it he realised that it no longer looked quite so high as it used to when he clambered up it to pick the fruit before the crows ransacked the tree. 'And over there, Mamma used to grow cucumbers. There were so many at harvest time that I was allowed to eat as many as I wanted whilst I collected them. Grandpappa used to put a bottle around some of the small cucumbers and let them grow bigger. Then he would cut them off the vine and place a small amount of vodka at the bottom of the bottle, which he would light and then quickly seal the top. In this way they kept fresh until Christmas and we served them as a special treat in our apartment in the centre.'

They were about to turn back to the coast when a big cloud suddenly made the shady area under the trees quite dark. Quite unexpectedly, big raindrops began to fall. Janis grabbed Hilkka's hand and quickly led her further up the path and then through a gap in the fence. After a short walk through some bushes they came to a small hut with big windows and a double door, which he tried. It opened and they went in. The hut was full of chairs and a wooden sun lounger that he remembered his mother using in the garden. It soon stopped raining but Janis suggested that they stay to eat the picnic that they had brought with them in a knapsack borrowed from Ginta.

The sun came out and the hut was cosy. Janis moved some of the furniture around and they sat on the sun lounger with its padded base and pillow.

'Welcome to my home,' Janis said as he poured two glasses of Rigas Balsams, 'it is very strange being back. Everything is familiar but it seems such a long time ago as well.' He explained that the summerhouse belonged to his grandparents and they used to spend every summer with them until he was about eight. Janis said, 'Grandpappa kept bees but when Grandmamma died he stopped coming to the summerhouse and we had to give the bees away.'

Janis lay back on the pillow and Hilkka rested her head on his chest. As they relaxed into each other, he asked Hilkka what her first memory was. She thought about this for a while and said, 'I think it was a horse in the village being shot. Cars in our village were quite rare when I was a child and most people had horse and carts. I remember the day that a big truck came into the market square. It must have backfired as I heard something that sounded like a whip being cracked. A horse tethered to a rail shied and tried to jump up over a raised platform. It collapsed and couldn't get up. I noticed that the poor animal's leg was at a distorted angle. I was with my mother and she pushed us away from the scene when a policeman came over. We were walking away when I heard another crack. I remembered the scene and reminded my mother some years later of it. Mother explained that the horse had to be shot as it had broken its leg. I remember crying until I fell asleep that night.' Janis involuntarily touched his shin.

Janis realised that they both had had early experience of death but such everyday experiences could never have prepared them for what they would later have to deal with. Janis tried to lighten the recollections by recalling one of his first memories of being by the sea. 'I remember once when a man came up to us when I was with Mamma and Ginta. He said that he had lost his false teeth in the water. Ginta and I started to laugh because we had never seen a man before without any teeth, but Mamma made us be quiet. We tried to find them for him but he had to go home empty mouthed. The next day we were walking by the shore and we saw a pair of false teeth lying there, which must have been washed in by the waves. We took them home but the man never came back for them.' Hilkka quickly added, 'Perhaps he has only eaten soft fruit for the last twenty years!' They both laughed.

After a pause, Janis asked, 'You shouted out in your sleep last night, what were you dreaming about? It sounded like you were frightened.' Hilkka furrowed her brow and looked pensive for a moment and then replied, 'Yes, I had almost forgotten about it but I had a very vivid dream last night. I was with my whole family and we were walking in the forest in Finland. I remember in real life going with them once and they played a trick on me. They disappeared all at once behind trees and I was suddenly alone in this forest. One minute, I was happy and safe and then I was alone in a dark place. It was only a few moments before I saw my sisters laughing, but to me it felt like an eternity. I was very angry and started to cry and my mother and father were quick to say sorry for playing a trick on me. But, in the dream they disappeared forever. One minute we were walking and talking and the sun was shining and then suddenly I was left completely, scared and alone.'

Janis stroked his wife's hair and said, 'Yes, of course that would be really frightening.' Then Hilkka asked, 'And what of your dreams, I often hear you say a name or something like that.' Janis suddenly felt a chill go through him and quickly replied, 'I do have dreams but I can't really remember them.' There was no way that he was going to tell Hilkka that Velichko often visited at night. 'But what of future dreams?' he asked.

Hilkka thought for a short while and said, 'One day I would like to show you my hometown and take you to all the lovely places that I know. We can go sailing on the lake and walking in the forest. I would like to show you my school and father's sanatorium. I would like to visit my mother's grave and we can put some flowers there.' Janis replied, 'That's my dream too, and why not? It is part of the Soviet Union. One day we might be free to travel.'

After a short while, Hilkka asked, 'How do you feel about me being here?' 'I feel like it's a bit of a fairy-tale and I have to pinch myself to see if it is real,' Janis replied.

'Do you love me?' Hilkka asked as they lay back together looking up at the beams. Janis replied, 'I do,' and realised that he had not said anything as true as this before.

A Life in the Day

On the 20th March 1950, Janis woke around five thirty. He could have slept longer as his shift did not commence until eight o'clock but he found it impossible to sleep on. Each day from five a dull ache in his leg would build and prevent further sleep. When he put his weight on his leg first thing in the morning, pain would shoot up his shin but after a while it would ease. Janis limped to the door, opened it and headed to the kitchen. It was light outside but there was still snow on the ground and the sky was overcast. The gloom in the kitchen matched Janis' mood. Signs of Oswalds' nocturnal activities were evident in the form of unwashed plates and greasy pans.

Hilkka was up and in a dressing gown when Janis brought in two cups of tea. Jauntily as he could muster, he asked, 'What's on the agenda today?' Hilkka replied, 'Well first, I am meeting the Finnish Ambassador for breakfast and then I am coming back to wash your clothes.'

By six thirty Janis was waiting by the tram stop on Exporta Street. Wet snow had started to fall quite heavily. He looked over towards the docks, which every day seemed to be growing bigger. New cranes could be seen and large buildings were going up. The tram was already full when he got on and it headed towards the centre. He made this trip daily but never got used to the mouldy smell of damp clothing and unwashed bodies. After waiting for a connecting tram to take him from the centre to Hospital Number 1 on the corner of Lenin Street and Red Army Street, Janis arrived at his place of work around seven twenty, which provided the opportunity to have a chat with one of his colleagues who was on a similar shift.

This morning, Janis was on the same shift as Uldis and they greeted each other in the now traditional manner of, 'Good morning, *Tovarisch*, comrade.' They discussed the big news that had occurred three nights previously of a senior party official disappearing from the hospital. He had been admitted with a suspected burst appendix and then that night he had gone. He had not been discharged but had simply vanished. Janis said, 'We will have to ask Alexey what has happened.' Alexey worked in the canteen and was considered suspicious as he was always smiling. As Janis mentioned Alexey's name he shut one eye in reference to the joke that had been told a few weeks before. It had made him laugh even though there was no punch line as such. The joke was about how you identify an NKVD man. The answer was that, whilst they sit in cafes watching people, NKVD officers always have a spoon in their teacup and when they lift it up the spoon goes into their eye; hence they walk around with one eye shut. Now, simply by closing one eye, Janis and his colleagues had a signal to identify an NKVD informer.

The work rota meant that Janis had to clean the orthopaedic ward that morning. This seemed to be always full of Russians who had fallen at work or been crushed with machinery. Janis realised that even if he never went outside of the hospital it would, nevertheless, be clear that Riga was in the process of being industrialised. The ward was always busy and to Janis it felt like a field hospital. Men were patched and splinted and sent back to the front. As Janis swept his mop back and forth, he noticed one young man with a plaster cast around his left shin. Janis' thoughts went back to the time that he spent in Grandmother Metusiha's house as she kneaded his shinbone back into shape. Although he was only dimly aware of what was happening, he marvelled about how she had worked. Without medical training, she had definitely saved his life and had mended his leg as well as any doctor in a well-equipped hospital could have done.

The cleaning rota took Janis down the corridors and stairs of the hospital and by one o'clock he was able to join the nurses in the canteen for a lunch of solyanka soup and fried fish. He sat by himself. The Soviet rallying cry of 'Workers of the World Unite' had not found its way into the hospital and the rules of the hierarchy extended to whom you were able to sit by. Janis once took his plate to a table occupied by three nurses and was impolitely told to sit elsewhere.

After lunch Janis returned to his cleaning duties, this time on a ward that contained people either waiting for or recovering from surgery. With his brown coat and on the brown floors, he merged into the scenery and was able to overhear the Soviet propaganda and anti-Semitic comments that had replaced the dialogue and banter as Janis remembered the conversations he once heard as a patient.

In a corner of the ward two Latvians were in animated discussion. One was almost hanging out of his bed as he spelled out to the other, 'In order to turn a peasant society into an industrialised nation, countless material and human sacrifices are necessary. Enthusiasm is not enough. They need to be made to accept the change and a powerful authority is required.' It seemed that he was talking to the converted as his neighbour did not argue but added, 'Yes, if a few million people have to perish in the process people will forgive Stalin.' Not wanting to be outdone in support of the cause, the other man added, 'A great aim needs great energy and could be drawn from peasants only by harshness.' Both lay back happy that they had got their points across. Hearing some Latvians supporting the new regime no longer surprised Janis.

A little later, Janis overheard a conversation between two Russians. It was not particularly in hushed tones because it was about Jews and if you were being rude about them this was acceptable. One man in a nasal tone sounded off, 'Jews will never fit in because they have never understood the idea of a leader. All other nations learnt to submit to Rome. Oh no, not the Jews. It is their tragedy never to have a nation and it comes from not having a God's representative on earth. They have no Christ or Mohammed. For them there is no absolute authority on earth. It is only the superior Jews that can commune directly with God! To keep a nation you need to submit to a supreme leader.' The other man nodded and concurred, 'You are quite right Vladamir, really, there is no place for them.'

Article 58

The rest of Janis' shift was spent unloading a consignment of medical supplies that had recently arrived from Moscow and taking the nappies from the maternity ward to the laundry.

By six fifteen Janis had finished his shift and waited for the tram to take him home. The wet snow had turned into a persistent drizzle and after a short time the rain began to run off the brim of his hat. The tram duly arrived and he climbed up the steps and into the fug with its distinct and powerful odour. Apart from the clatter of the tram and the rumble of traffic over the cobbles there was no noise. No one spoke. Everyone looked down. Half way home the tram braked suddenly and a women stood heavily on Janis' toe. Even then there was no utterance apart from a grunt by Janis.

On arriving home, Janis tried to sound jollier than he actually felt when he asked, 'Hilkka, how are you? What sort of day have you had?' 'Hilkka replied, 'I am quite fine. The Ambassador was out so I had a walk around the centre.' After she had given Janis some tea she added, 'I went into the Orthodox Church today. I know that it is now a meeting place and café but it still has some atmosphere. I pretended that I lit a candle.'

Janis quickly recapped his day and then focused on the incident in the tram. He complained, 'The soul of Riga has been ripped out. I remember people laughing in the hospital and on the streets. Mamma taught us that if you bump into people you should apologise. Now, no one makes eye contact anymore let alone say sorry. It is as if not noticing anyone is the same as not

183

being noticed. A grey blanket has settled everywhere.' Janis realised that this was simply depressing talk and vowed to himself that in the future he would not burden Hilkka with such mundane complaints.

Janis talked about the disappearance in the night of the senior party member. It prompted him to ask, 'I wonder how we escaped being deported?' Hilkka thought about the question and said, 'When you are the lowest of the low, there is a chance that you fall off the bottom of the list. You are an enemy of the people and an invalid. I am a captured Finn without any documentation. It is possibly too much trouble for someone to start a file.' Janis mused on the answer. He never considered himself an invalid and hesitated in his reply. Eventually he said, 'Yes, now give the poor invalid a kiss.' Any passion that may have developed was extinguished, not this time by Oswalds banging on the wall, but by the Russian couple starting one of their frequent rows. Predictably it started with the women shouting God knows what. The words were slurred and muffled. Then there was a great crash accompanied by swearing followed by silence.

The Conveyor

One evening in early March 1951 a man wearing a trench coat and thick scarf knocked on the door of Janis' room. He introduced himself to Janis, who was there with Hilkka, as a clerk working in the Ministry of the Interior. He spoke Latvian with a heavy Russian accent. The man made an attempt at being friendly by apologising for his poor Latvian. He explained that, although he had lived in Russia for a long time, his family was Latvian and he had returned to help build Soviet Latvia. Janis asked him then to speak Russian so that Hilkka could also understand the conversation. The clerk looked coldly at Janis as if his offer of cordial relationship had been shunned.

Janis was asked to go outside with the man. When he saw the look between Janis and Hilkka he said, 'There is no truck waiting for you.'

Janis walked for a while with the man. When he stopped to take a cigarette packet out of his pocket Janis noticed the gun holster and was reminded of the time when he had been approached to be an informer in Siberia. He knew then what this little chat was about. This time there was no running away. He duly listened to the offer that was made. Before he had a chance to say anything the man said, 'Think about it, I'll come back.'

When he returned to their room, Hilkka asked what

the man had wanted. Janis said, 'He just asked the same old questions' Janis felt cold and that something had changed in him. This deceit was added to the small list of things that he kept from Hilkka.

Janis had spent less than a year back in Riga and had begun to think of the possibility of having a normal existence. This was all threatened again and it seemed that his wife could not have returned at a more unsettling time. There was such malicious action compounded by random acts that Janis felt sure that they would be separated again.

Refusing to be an informer surely meant certain deportation. Then he thought of his father who must have died because he refused to collaborate. How could he offend his memory by becoming an informer? Yet, he pondered on this very act.

The next day, and just as Janis had finished a shift at work, two NKVD officers were waiting for him by the exit of the hospital used by the workers. The guard at the door pointed to Janis and he was arrested. The two officers escorted him to a car with black windows and he was taken to the 'Corner Building'. Everyone knew the interrogation centre that got its name by being on the intersection of Lenin Street and Engels Street. After basic details were taken, Janis was escorted down a corridor with rows of battleship grey cell doors.

The guards unlocked one of the grey doors and Janis was pushed inside the brightly lit cell. He immediately had a moment of panic for he saw that two of the men in there had terrible looking tattoos. 'So here we find the urki,' Janis said to himself. In total there were ten people in the cell and the two tattooed criminals took up half the cell as they sprawled out and made themselves comfortable on the bunks. The others sat in the rest of the overcrowded cell. Four people sat on the two other bunk beds but the rest were on the floor. A space was made there for Janis.

As soon as Janis had settled down the criminals sat up and one clambered down from his bunk. Janis felt his heart thump in his chest. The man came over and stood over Janis who noticed the crudely drawn tattoo on his hands and knuckles. The criminal demanded tobacco. When he did not answer the man stooped to search Janis' jacket pocket. Janis remembered what his workmate, Kaspars, had said, 'Show no fear', and he surprised himself when he told the criminal to move away – using the best Russian expletives that he could muster.

The tattooed man took a step back in surprise and then without further hesitation thrust his two fingers at Janis' eyes. Janis recalled what he had been told of the methods of the urki and was expecting this old tactic of blinding people. He caught the criminal's fingers just in front of his own face.

The hard physical work in Siberia had created real muscle in Janis' right arm and he squeezed the fingers of the man as hard as he could. One twist would have broken bones but he refrained from this and let the hand go. The criminal put his crushed hand under his arm and went back to his bunk. Here, clearly, was a problem that needed some consideration. Janis fully expected the other to join in but he was surprised when he did not move. What he uttered though was far more frightening, 'You are the hare.'

Janis was extremely worried that later he would be awoken with a knife in his chest and decided that he could not afford to go to sleep that night.

As it happened he did not go to sleep that night but that was for a different reason.

A few hours after the incident with the urki the guards came into the cell and demanded that Janis follow them to a separate room. Never had he imagined that he would be relieved to be following prison guards.

Article 58

The guards took Janis to an interrogation room with two doors, an inner and outer one, which had to be opened together before they entered. The back of the inside door was covered with a padded oilcloth and Janis wondered if this was for sound insulation. The room had a desk and two chairs with a lamp over one of the chairs, which the guards made Janis sit on. Then they left him alone. He was still feeling happy to be out of the cell and away from the criminals when in came two men dressed in grey, ill fitting suits. One of the men, who was unusually stick like with thin, pallid lips, started what was obviously going to be another interrogation. This covered the familiar territory and Janis gave his usual replies. Then the stick said to the one waiting by the door, 'Put him on the conveyor.'

The conveyor turned out to be a deceptively simple form of torture. Janis was interrogated all day. The same questions were repeated and Janis gave the same answers. Then the stick left and a guard replaced him. Janis felt tired and his head nodded forward. The guard suddenly shouted that it was forbidden to go to sleep.

Janis was allowed to visit the toilet. There was a screen of sorts but it was only waist height and a guard remained with him at all times. Sitting down he put his heavy head in his hands and the guard screamed again for him to sit upright. Back in the cell the guard constantly awoke him and threatened him with punishment cells or worse if he fell asleep.

The interrogation room was in the basement and daylight eventually appeared in a tiny window at the top of the wall. Later in the morning the questioning started again after the stick had asked in a jaunty manner whether Janis had had a good night.

There began to be periods when Janis suddenly had no recollection of what had happened in the last minutes. Then larger and larger chunks of time dropped out of his memory. As the hours progressed he felt himself get loose and less coherent. Eventually the interrogator left and Janis had only a guard for company. Janis tried to sit bolt upright to bring back some form of coherent thought and when this failed he tried to sleep by also sitting up straight. However, any giveaway nod brought a sharp rebuke from the guard.

The odd snippet of sleep was too little and Janis felt that this night was the longest one that he had ever endured. Thoughts, half formed, passed through his mind. He found that he was unable to hold onto anything; thoughts, memories, fantasies began to come uncontrollably.

Janis recalled a march that he had seen in Riga recently after the occupation. Then he saw himself in the crowd waving the Red Flag and shouting communist slogans.

A jumble of nonsensical thoughts came and then Janis was in his family home on the fashionable Alberts Street. His father was back early from work and his mother was in tears. Janis asked 'Pappa, why is Mamma crying?' and his father said 'All the apartments are being nationalised. The Siegalmans have been evicted to make way for a senior Russian

Officer.' Janis then imagined he was sitting in the front room of the Siegalmans' apartment wearing his Pioneers uniform with red scarf and smoking a large cigar.

Janis recalled the time when all the school clubs were closed down, even the Chess Club. Everyone of Janis' age and below had to join the Pioneers.

For a while, memories flooded back of happy times in Janis' childhood. He recalled one summer's evening when he was on a camping expedition with his classmates from school. There was a great bonfire and around it the boys sat singing songs and playing games. He remembered the Latvian flag being flown on the campsite and of the boys taking it in turns to keep guard. Then the scene changed. He saw his friends standing and saluting the Red Flag and talking in Russian. They turned to Janis and with ghoul-like faces shouted at him, 'Article 58 – treason towards the motherland.'

Another memory came of his school friends all going to church in the first summer of the occupation. They had known that this was really disapproved of and although not particularly religious were doing this as an act of defiance. Then, suddenly Janis saw himself in church listening to Stalin at the pulpit delivering a speech, 'The sins of the father are suffered unto the seventh generation.' He heard Stalin as if he was in the room. Suddenly the church was overridden by rats running through and Stalin shouted, 'Eradicate the vermin.' Then the image faded and his thoughts became even more jumbled.

Janis sat bolt upright. 'What are you doing here?' he demanded as he saw the dripping wet figure of Velichko enter the room. Velichko's face was paper white and his watery eyes were now blood shot. 'You let me drown, you worthless piece of shit. How do you sleep at night with the death of two people on your conscience?' Velichko rushed at Janis and by closing his eyes he managed to avoid the mountainous arm that lunged for his throat. Shutting his eyes brought a strong rebuke from the guard, 'Sleep and you will be punished.'

The interrogation began again next day, still without Janis having had any sleep. His mind was terribly woozy as if badly hung over. Was it the stick or himself who had said that he was a weed that needed to be removed? Yes, it could be true that he was an enemy of the people. He had hoped that the Germans won the war. Thoughts came and merged. Who was asking the questions and who was responding became blurred.

Suddenly the interrogation was over. Janis with his few belongings was released and he was left blinking on the street getting used to the weak morning sun. He, at first, was unsure as to how to get home.
Dazed, Janis arrived back at the apartment, which was greeted with huge relief by Hilkka. She had had no word about Janis and had begun to suspect that he had been deported or worse. Janis lay on the bed fully clothed and went to sleep for the next twelve hours.

The next day, the man who said that he was a clerk at the Ministry of the Interior returned and again requested that Janis accompany him for a walk. Outside he said, 'I understand that you have had a taste of the NKVD's interview procedure.' The man smiled as he said this and Janis realised that his trip to The Corner House had been part of a softening up process. If he did not agree to be an informer, there could be more of this to come, or, he would be sent back to Siberia as a prisoner along with his friends the urki.

'How can I help you?' were the hardest words that Janis had ever had to say.

Article 58

The Arts

The weather warmed, became hot at the height of the summer and cooled in autumn but life carried on much the same in 1951. There were some highlights and amongst them was a trip to Cinema Riga where The Battleship Potemkin was being shown. Janis was not keen to see the old film but its appeal was in the fact that it was being screened at his favourite cinema and the Director had a connection to his family's old residence in Alberts Street.

It was a late summer's afternoon when Janis and Hilkka strolled through Vermanis Park in the centre of Riga towards the cinema. The roses were in their second flush and everything was neat. The path had been swept early in the morning and it still looked tidy. Ladies in summer dresses sauntered along and office workers dawdled in their efforts to deliver important papers. Riga appeared, as it had always seemed to Janis, pretty and feminine.

As the couple strolled, Janis wondered why the Soviets had changed the name of 'The Splendid Palace' to 'Cinema Riga'. 'Does everything have to look and sound grey?' he pondered. The Splendid Palace was, as its name suggested, a splendid picture-palace. It was built in the art nouveau style with interesting plaster reliefs and it had a grand chandelier in the auditorium. When Janis was around the age of twelve he used to go to 'Saturday morning pictures' and as the couple approached the cinema, hand in hand, Janis recalled the mayhem that ensued on these occasions. The audience would join in with every chase or adventure and the shouts and cheers of his contemporaries drowned out the sound of the piano when they showed the silent movies.

Janis showed Hilkka around the vestibule and anteroom of the cinema and as a very special treat they bought themselves some tea in the café situated downstairs. The ornate plasterwork of stylised trees looked even more amazing than when he had seen it as a child. A buzzer sounded to signify that the film was about to start and the couple took their seats in the auditorium.

When the name of the Director, Sergei Eisenstein, was shown on the screen Janis leaned over and whispered to Hilkka, 'His father, Mikhail, designed our house in Alberts' Street.' Seeing Eisenstein's name was one of the main reasons for coming but Janis, with his hand clasped to Hilkka's, settled back and watched the rest of the grainy black and white film.

On the way back through the park, Janis asked Hilkka what she thought of the film. Hilkka quickly said, 'For such an old film, it was really well done. The scene where the tsar's soldiers in their white summer tunics march down a seemingly endless flight of steps in a rhythmic, machine-like fashion, firing volleys into a crowd is amazing. I can see why it is shown everywhere. It is a heroic revolutionary tale of the overthrow of the tsar. But Jani, the tsar's soldiers have been replaced by the Red Army and the NKVD. Nothing much has really changed.' Janis looked around. This was the sort of thing that must not be overheard.

Late one evening, Janis and his sister had the opportunity to talk together in Ginta's attic. Janis spoke quietly, 'Ginta, have you noticed how Hilkka is becoming sadder and more withdrawn? I am really worried about her. Life is incredibly boring for her and living here must be squashing her soul. I am sure that she would like a baby but it is not happening. And God forbid, what would happen if we did have one? We have no spare room and Oswalds is no neighbour for a child to have. Is there anything that you can think of that could help? I am desperately worried. She used to sing when we were in Siberia and now we rarely do or we risk Oswalds banging on the wall. She used to like painting but we can't afford the materials and places on a course are denied.' Ginta replied, 'Jani, I have seen how Hilkka is going into herself but for now I have no ideas as to how to help.'

Later in the week Ginta knocked on Janis' door after a late performance at the Opera House. Janis opened the door and Ginta said quickly, 'I know it's late so I won't keep you both up but I have brought some paper and some pencils from the rehearsal studio. I wondered whether you, Hilkka, would be interested in using them?' Hilkka thanked Ginta for her kindness and put the paper and pens in a drawer. When Ginta had closed the door and left, Hilkka turned to Janis and asked, 'If I guess correctly, you have prompted this. Have you said something to Ginta about me?' He immediately replied, 'Hilkka, yes, I talked to Ginta the other evening about you. I said that I was worried. Life is dreadfully boring for you and I asked her if she had any ideas.' Hilkka responded, 'Don't worry about me, I am stronger than I look.'

Later that week, Ginta again knocked on the door. This time she asked, 'Tomorrow, would you both like to come to a rehearsal of a new opera? Its première is coming up later in the month. It's by Shostakovich and is called Lady Macbeth of Mtsensk. I know the Director and he has allowed me to take a few friends to see the rehearsal of a scene or two.' Hilkka's face lit up. 'Yes, please. That would be so lovely, thank you.'

Janis and Hilkka met Ginta at the back of the Opera House and she ushered them into the building via the stage door. Janis had been a few times to the Opera House but never before back stage. The vast cathedral-like space into which scenery could be winched impressed him. Seeing all the lighting and cabling, Janis commented to his sister, 'I can't believe how technical this all looks. From the other side of the curtain, it is so different.' Ginta said, 'Opera is a metaphor for life and this is just part of that.' Janis was surprised at just how profound his sister could be at times.

After a brief tour backstage, Ginta took Janis and Hilkka to their seats at the back of the stalls and she sat with them. Janis looked around the gilded auditorium and asked Ginta, 'Do you remember when we were last here together?' It seems like it could have been just yesterday when we saw Cinderella with Mamma and Pappa. Was that where we sat?' Janis pointed upwards towards seats on their left. Ginta replied, 'Yes, it was. It was the first time that I saw Cinderella and I have danced in it since. Prokofiev is my favourite composer.'

A few more people took seats in the stalls and then in came the Director with his assistant. The Director looked over and gave the slightest of waves towards Ginta. Janis wondered whether there was anything between the two of them and then thought, 'Why not, Ginta is pretty, young and single.' Ginta whispered the Director's name, Mikhail, to Janis and Hilkka. In the orchestra pit a discordant noise built as instruments were tuned and tested. Ginta leaned over and said, 'Some people can't tell the difference between this and Shostakovich's music!' They laughed and wondered what they were about to hear.

The curtain was already drawn back and onto the stage came the singers. The Director addressed them from the stalls, 'This afternoon we are going to concentrate on Act Four. Katarina and Sergei are on their way to exile in Siberia after being convicted of killing Katarina's husband. Katarina bribes a guard to allow her to meet Sergei, her lover. Now, Katarina,' The Director addressed the main singers on the stage, 'I want you to look and sound desperate and Sergei, I want you to be callous and harsh. You are a user of women. Be ruthless in your seduction of Sonyetka, one of the prisoners.'

The opera singers took their places and the orchestra started. Janis had never before heard a sound like it. As it went on he whispered to Ginta, 'This music is the essence of Russia, messy yet beautiful. It is discordant and magnificent.'

Twice, the Director interrupted the proceedings. First,

he asked Sonyetka to be coarser and then he asked Katarina to be more in a rage when she pushes Sonyetka into an icy river. In one of the interruptions, Ginta leaned across and said, 'The Director is taking a big risk, Stalin doesn't like this opera.'

At the finale, Janis wanted to stand and clap. The music and the scene of prisoners being transported to Siberia enraptured him. But as this was only a rehearsal he felt inhibited. All he could do was sit for a while in silence.

Ginta was due to meet a friend in the centre after the rehearsal and so Janis and Hilkka made their way home without her. They did not speak much on the tram but in their room Janis and Hilkka became quite talkative, 'Ginta is right,' Hilkka said, 'opera is a metaphor for life but it can never capture the truth. It cannot show you just how cold the water is that Katarina and Sonyetka plunged into. It cannot show you the depth of a person's despair or loneliness.' Janis thought about what Hilkka had said and remarked, 'Individual experience can never be truly shared; most of our feelings cannot be put into words. That is what makes opera so powerful; music comes closer to expressing the soul.' Later on, he wondered whether he had missed the point of what Hilkka was really trying to say to him. Did he not understand her or her situation? Was she saying that she was lonely and in despair? He thought about saying something but let it go.

Hilkka went out of the room to make some tea and when she reappeared she asked, 'Jani, would you like to see my drawings?' Janis looked surprised, as

Hilkka had not mentioned using the paper and pencils given to her by Ginta. The drawings were of a lakeshore and a farmhouse in Siberia. Janis was surprised just how good they were and showed his delight with a big hug and a kiss.

Two days after Janis and Hilkka had accompanied Ginta to see the rehearsal of the opera, Ginta knocked on their door, again late in the evening. When Janis opened the door he immediately noticed that her eyes were bloodshot and puffy and could tell that she had been crying. 'Goodness, what's the matter?' he asked and ushered his sister into the room. With her head slightly bowed, Ginta said, 'The opera has been cancelled. There will be no opening of Lady Macbeth of Mtsensk. Stalin has said that he will shut any opera house that plays Shostakovich's anti-revolutionary noise.'

Article 58

Article 58

Life as an Informer

Janis' duties as an informer were simple; to report anyone involved in anti-Soviet discussions, distribution of counter-revolutionary pamphlets or literature and anyone found in possession of foreign currency or illegal weapons. The task was clear enough but it was not simple. Janis did not seek clarification on what constituted anti-Soviet discussions or what came under the category of counter-revolutionary literature as he knew that almost everything would be included from telling jokes of Stalin to reading the bible.

One evening, whilst waiting for his tram home, a man in a trench coat stood next to Janis, tapped him on the arm and said, 'Did you drop this?' The man passed Janis a slip of paper. By the time that he had looked down at the paper and up again the man had merged into the waiting crowd. Janis decided not to catch the next tram and instead he took the paper to look at it under the glow of a streetlight. The paper simply had a typed date and time and address on it. Janis got on the next tram with a mounting sense of unease. Despite listening to conversations at the hospital he had not heard any anti-Soviet discussion or found any counter-revolutionary pamphlets and had nothing to report. However, he knew that as an informer and especially one who had the threat of deportation hanging over his head he needed to come up with something to keep the NKVD happy.

Article 58

On the prescribed date and time, Janis arrived at the address that he had been given. He stood outside the block that once would have been smart residential properties but now had been turned into non-descript offices. He rang the bell of the address that he had been given and he heard the bolt of the ornately carved wooden door being released. Janis decided not to use the rather old looking lift, which ran up the centre of the staircase but instead walked up two flights of stairs. The door of the office he was looking for was already slightly ajar and when he pushed it, it opened to reveal the smiling face of the man who had introduced himself as a clerk in the Ministry of the Interior. In what seemed to Janis to be an overly familiar manner he said, 'Jani, welcome. Would you like some tea?' Janis declined the offer and they went into a small office with a simple desk and two chairs with a lamp over one of the chairs into which Janis was directed to sit. He immediately became concerned that he would be put back on the 'conveyor'.

'So, Jani, what have you to report?' asked the clerk. Janis could feel the sweat forming on his brow and it took him a few seconds to form the word in response, 'Nothing.' The clerk gave an ironic sounding laugh, 'Sorry, you are telling me that in a large, busy hospital you have heard nothing suspicious. Everyone has behaved as good Soviet citizens and there has been no anti-revolutionary talk.' The clerk's eyes and thin lips narrowed. 'What! I simply don't believe you.' He had come close to Janis' face and with the force of the utterance flecks of spit hit Janis in the eye. The clerk softened his voice and went back to a slightly more chatty tone, 'Janis, do you not know that a revolution is underway. The tsars' Kulaks have been booted out.

Agriculture is collectivised. Now we are on the path to industrialisation where the worker is the most important cog in the machine. Are you telling me that there are no dissenters? No one with a vested interest to keep the old order has mentioned anything? Unbelievable! We need to root out the reactionaries. Nothing good can be made when there are people around who want to take us back to their idea of the good old days. There are weeds in the garden that need to be uprooted.'

The clerk continued, 'Unless you are keen to see the inside of a prison cell again, I suggest that you redouble your efforts. I have nothing to report, is simply not acceptable.' Janis realised that by the time that he was summoned again he had better have some real news.

Janis slept badly over the next few nights. On the third morning of not being able to sleep past four o'clock Hilkka asked Janis if there was anything that was troubling him. He gave the excuse of his leg aching more than usual. At least that day there was something to look forward to. It was Sunday and they had been invited by Ginta to see her perform as the Fairy Godmother in Cinderella. The Opera House was such a complete contrast to their daily lives; it had a magic of its own. There, the couple felt that they were transported to a different world. Janis remembered going to see Cinderella with his parents and how everyone had returned home in high spirits. He thought, 'This is the lift that we both need.'

Ginta had left for the Opera House early that day and as the performance was a matinée, Janis and Hilkka set off just after lunch. It was April and although there were no flowers or blossoms out in the garden outside the Opera House, they sat for a while on a park bench there enjoying the strong sunlight before venturing inside. Ginta had been allocated two seats in the dress circle and, after depositing their coats in the cloakroom, they made their way there with a feeling of rising excitement

Janis remembered the buzz and chatter that there had been before the performance that he had come to see with his parents and Ginta. Now it seemed more subdued. The numbers of uniforms in the audience made it look more like a military affair. Nevertheless, Janis was glad to be there especially because he was about to see his sister perform for the first time.

To the resounding sound of Prokofiev's music the curtain opened and the ballet began. Janis did not have to wait long before Ginta was on stage. She appeared as an old beggar woman asking for shelter. The sisters and mother tried to chase her off but Cinderella offered her a place by the kitchen fire and an old pair of slippers. The beggar thanked her for her kindness and departed, leaving the preparations for the ball to resume. Janis was amazed at how well Ginta played the beggar and how, through dance, she captured the decrepit stance and gait. Then Ginta revealed herself as the Fairy Godmother. Janis had never seen his sister looking so radiant. Ginta turned the slippers into glass dancing shoes and granted Cinderella's wish of going to the ball. Janis whispered to Hilkka, 'How beautiful Ginta looks.'

Ginta summoned the fairies of Spring, Summer,

Autumn and Winter. Then she turned Cinderella's rags into a beautiful dress, a pumpkin and mice into a carriage with horses, and grasshoppers and dragonflies into a retinue of footmen. Janis thought that this was the most beautiful thing that he had ever seen.

There was a break in which Janis and Hilkka joined with the audience to promenade arm in arm around the anteroom at the back of the dress circle. Janis asked Hilkka, 'Do you like this circling?' and she replied, 'Yes, it is a chance to see and be seen. Everyone looks very fine indeed.' Janis was sure that everyone was fine except himself and he tried to walk as best he could without limping.

The couple could not afford the cost of a drink but were uplifted enough by the ballet. They talked about how well Ginta played the part of the Fairy Godmother.

Ginta made her reappearance in the final act. The Prince had almost given up finding the beautiful girl at the ball when the remaining slipper fell from Cinderella's pocket in front of him. Overjoyed, Ginta transported the two away to a secret garden, where they confessed their love for one another and were married. The curtain closed to great applause. Janis and Hilkka saved their strongest clapping for when Ginta came onto the stage to receive her flowers.

Janis and Hilkka were elated when they left the Opera House. Not only was the Opera House a gilded palace, which was so different to their squalid room, the ballet had also taken them to an opulent world where love overcame ambition and jealousy.

The couple sat hand in hand on the way back but with every bump and rattle of the tram taking them home, Janis' spirits deflated.

Janis suddenly made the connection between Cinderella and Hilkka's position. Cinderella had to work all day sweeping and cleaning and could not go to the ball. He thought, 'What is my Cinderella doing all day? What ball has she been refused to go to? If the Soviets had not invaded Finland what would her life be like now? Surely, as a beautiful, intelligent Finn she would be having a completely different life. She would be dancing and singing and maybe a mother. What has she been robbed of? Who knows, but what is for sure, she would not be living with a cripple in a hovel.' Janis had made himself quite miserable by the time they got off the tram. He wondered whether Hilkka had been thinking along the same lines as she had become very still and quiet. When they got back to their house, a sailor pushed past them as he hurriedly left the rooms of Oswalds' daughter.

After the elation and deflation of the ballet, Janis soon got back into a routine and began to think about what he could tell the clerk. He had to give him something but people repeating Stalinist propaganda and anti-Semitic views was not news. He could not think of denouncing his colleagues for telling jokes about Stalin. After all, that meant denouncing himself. Janis donned his brown coat and listened out. He smiled at the thought of finding a spy trying to contact the West by radio from under his bedcovers.

There were no more demands to visit the clerk for the next three months. Janis had almost begun to think that the authorities had lost interest when a piece of paper was again slipped into his hands at the tram stop on his way home. A cold sweat built quickly on his forehead.

Janis duly arrived at the appointed time. 'Your report,' demanded the clerk. His tone was not friendly this time. It was a command and not a request. Janis said, 'Each Tuesday there is a meeting of a counter-revolutionary cell in the store in E wing of the hospital on the fourth floor. I am not sure what is said but the meeting lasts approximately one hour and the door is locked.' Janis was told to write this down. After he had done so, the clerk dismissed him with a wave of the hand. Janis hoped that when acted on, his information would appear to be flawed and he would not be used again.

Janis was not on duty when the NKVD knocked on the door of the store and made those inside open up. The day after, he met Uldis in the changing area who was just finishing his nightshift. Uldis had heard that senior doctors and some nurses had been hauled off to the Corner House and that the Stores Manager has been arrested for theft. Uldis concluded, 'He'll get a ten year stretch at least.' Janis felt his stomach turn.

Pneumonia

Hilkka carried on with her drawing but she showed them to Janis less frequently. In fact, everything had become less frequent. Janis knew that the pressure of being an informer had begun to change him. He was continually on edge. Now he understood more about the system, it was clear that there was even more randomness than he had previously imagined. When would there be a knock on the door from the NKVD confronting them with some trumped up charge?

The only thing that lifted the couple out of what seemed like a depression was the very occasional music concert.

In March 1952, Ginta again offered the couple tickets and this time it was to see the first performance of a new production of La Boheme. Ginta explained that her friend was directing the Opera. Janis had largely forgotten the roller coaster emotions brought on by seeing Cinderella and thanked his sister for the tickets. 'Of course, we will be delighted. Will you be sitting with us?' Ginta said that she would be attending the première but would be sitting with the Director himself.

The opera was later in the month and this gave Hilkka the opportunity to make a dress. When Hilkka told Janis that she wanted to make a dress for the occasion he said, 'You are woman with endless talents.' He recalled how Hilkka had mended his clothing and, just like his mother, had made things out of virtually nothing in Siberia. Although the weather might not be warm when they were due to go to the Opera, Hilkka made something that revealed her arms. Janis said that she would look especially beautiful in this.

The opening night came around soon enough and they were back at the Opera House. It felt like a home that they were returning to. Janis had saved up enough to buy two glasses of Russian champagne, which they sipped whilst looking out of the large windows overlooking the bare gardens. Janis felt happier than he had done in a long time. He could leave the job at the hospital with all its additional stresses behind for a while at least. Now, he was standing by the most beautiful woman in the room and in her new dress he thought that she looked even more attractive than normal. He whispered to her, 'I am the luckiest man in Riga,' and Hilkka gave his hand a small squeeze.

Soon Janis and Hilkka took their seats for the performance. They knew the story of how Rodolfo, a struggling writer and Mimì, a poor seamstress fall in love but they had not heard Puccini's music. Both were captivated by the whole opera.

The final act proved to be extremely emotional.

In the final act Rodolfo and Mimi remembered past happiness and their first meeting when their candles blew out and Rodolfo pretended that he had lost a key. Then suddenly, Mimì was overwhelmed by a coughing fit. She had pneumonia and was very sick. Rodolfo gave a gift of a fur muff to warm Mimì's hands and some medicine. Mimì gently thanked Rodolfo for the muff, reassured him that she was better and then died. Rodolfo rushed to Mimì's bed. Calling her name in anguish Rodolfo wept helplessly.

Both Janis and Hilkka took time to join in with the enthusiastic clapping that came with the curtain being drawn across the stage. Both of them wiped tears from their eyes and then came back to the present moment before beginning their applause.

Ginta had invited both Janis and Hilkka backstage for a celebration of the première but they worried that they might feel out of place. They decided to leave Ginta to enjoy herself with her friends and, after taking their coats from the cloakroom, they made their way onto the now dark streets. A cold wind had blown up since the afternoon and rain was in the air. Unusually, the couple had to wait a long time for their tram and by the time that it arrived the rain had developed into a fine downpour of the sort that soaked you completely. When they got back to their room they found that the communal heating had been turned off and both struggled to get warm.

The next day at work, Janis felt the benefit of going to the opera. The underlying anxiety of life was lessened. When he returned home in the evening he found Hilkka in bed. Anxiety flooded back.

Janis felt Hilkka's forehead. It was burning hot and she reported that she had felt unwell since mid-morning. Janis was suddenly in a panic. The women in his life had dealt with all the illnesses and he really did not know what to do. He ran up to Ginta's attic hoping that she would be in but it was soon clear that she was not yet home. Collecting himself, Janis thought that the only thing he could do was make some tea and keep the patient warm. The room felt cold and damp. The communal heating, it appeared, had been switched off for the summer months even though it was only some eleven degrees outside. After boiling water and making herbal tea, Janis added his coat to the blankets that covered Hilkka. When she drifted off to sleep he sat on a chair and worried.

It was late into the evening when Ginta returned home. Janis had been listening out for her and managed to stop her before she made her way up the stairs to her attic. In the room, he whispered, 'Is there anything that you can suggest?' Hilkka had awoken with the door being opened and interrupted with, 'Jani, don't fuss, I am stronger than I look.'

The next day, Janis was on a late shift and had time to make Hilkka comfortable before departing for work. It seemed that she was still burning up. Before he left, he asked his sister to call in to see Hilkka later in the afternoon and she replied 'Of course and Jani, bring some aspirin back from the hospital.'

Janis went about his duties at the hospital as best he could with his mind elsewhere. At the break he sought out a doctor whom he had come to recognise as both diligent and caring. 'Doctor, please could I have a moment?' Janis interrupted him en route to his next patient, 'I have a wife who is very sick at home. It might only be influenza but I am not sure what to do and if it is something worse I don't know how best to help her. Can I bring her to the hospital?' The doctor said, 'If you are worried, then you need to take her to the District Doctor.' Janis couldn't say anything more. To take Hilkka to the District doctor, she needed proper identification and a personal code, which had been denied.

Janis hurried home as fast as he could and cursed the tram system for making him wait at the connection. He felt completely powerless and cursed himself for not even being able to obtain any aspirin.

When Janis got back, Hilkka was hidden under more blankets after Ginta had donated hers. Still Hilkka complained of feeling cold, although her forehead felt to Janis that she must be consumed by a raging fire from within. He brewed more tea and with some resistance made Hilkka drink some of it.

Ginta returned home late into the evening and immediately knocked on Janis' door to find out news of the patient. Janis reported that there was a problem in getting any medical help. Ginta assured him that it must be simply a bad case of influenza and then said, 'Jani, if people at your hospital can't help, I have a name of a doctor who I know cares for all sorts whether they have a personal code or not. His name is Pauls Stradiņš and he works at a surgery in Ventspils Street in Agenskalns.'

In the night, Hilkka shouted out, 'Where are you, where are you? Please don't leave me.' Janis let her sleep on and wondered if she was dreaming again of being left alone in the forest by her family.

In the morning, Janis asked Ginta to go to the hospital to tell them that he would not be in that day. Later, Hilkka started to cough. At first it started as a little hiccupping and then it turned into a heavy throaty sound. Janis went out to buy some honey and mixed that into the tea.

The fever and the coughing got worse over the next day. Janis was beside himself. He simply could not let his wife get any worse. He put on his coat and set off for the address given to him by Ginta.

Janis crossed over the River Daugava, made his way to Ventspils Street and quickly located Dr. Stradiņš' surgery. When he pushed open the door he was confronted by a rather full waiting room and a stern-looking receptionist. He was not optimistic about getting an appointment but his request was met with a polite response and he was handed a number on a card.

Gradually the numbers in front of Janis whittled down and eventually it was his turn to see the doctor. When he entered the consulting room he was greeted with, '*Labdien*,' which surprised him as Latvian language was banned in the hospital. In Latvian, Janis quietly said, 'Doctor, I have come to see you about my wife. She does not have proper papers and I cannot take her to the District Doctor. She is too sick to be brought here. Can you help? I am a desperate man.' The doctor looked at Janis and then said quietly, 'Meet me at six o'clock here.' Janis breathed a deep sigh of relief.

Janis had an hour and a half to kill before the appointed time and used it to wander around the wooden buildings that made up this district. Some of the houses were built round a courtyard and he thought that, in times past, it could once have been very pleasant to live there. Now he was not sure and then realised that everywhere that he had known as pleasant had changed. Janis returned to the surgery before the appointed time and was relieved when he saw the doctor come out of the house on the dot of six.

Janis and the doctor travelled in silence on the tram and when the doctor was sitting down, Janis had the opportunity to look at him in some detail. He guessed that he was about fifty years of age but was surprised that he still looked rather fresh faced.

When they reached the room, Janis and the doctor could hear Hilkka coughing. Janis ushered him in and the doctor asked Hilkka how she was. All she managed to say was that she was dreadfully cold. Her temperature was taken and the doctor took out his stethoscope that he carried in a small bag and listened to her breathing. After a while, he said to Janis, 'Your wife has pneumonia. I will give you a prescription. As the hospital will not treat her without a personal code, the best that you can do is to make her as warm as possible. Try to keep the room heated but have plenty of ventilation. Keep her drinking; tea is as good as anything. If she gets worse come and get me.'

Janis wanted to hug the doctor but refrained from doing so. He knew that Dr. Stradiņš had taken a big risk coming to see a 'persona non grata'. Just after the doctor had departed Ginta arrived home. She came into the room and looked shocked when Janis told her of the diagnosis. Ginta immediately said that she would go for the prescription and asked Janis if there was anything else that he wanted her to get. His mind went back the final scene in La Boheme and was about to say, 'Please don't bring back a fur muff,' when he realised that he was being too dramatic. He just thanked Ginta and she left.

The medicine that the doctor prescribed was duly given. That night the coughing became more persistent and the next day there seemed little improvement. Hilkka rarely awoke and in a brief period of respite, Janis whispered to her, 'Don't leave me here, don't leave me here.' He was aware that he had said the exact same thing to his mother many years before.

Hilkka did not leave Janis. Bit by bit she recovered her strength and after two weeks was able to get out of bed.

After convalescing a while longer Janis took Hilkka out when the sky was blue. Although it was warm, Janis made her dress well. They took the tram to the centre of the city and by one of their favourite fountains they sat catching the rays of the late spring sunshine. After a while Janis asked Hilkka, 'Please be honest, how are you feeling and not just physically.' Hilkka replied, 'I will try to be honest....'

Hilkka thought about her reply to Janis' question for quite a while and then said, 'So I am here in Riga with you, my love, but it is not how I imagined it. I did not expect a flat of our own but I hoped we could have something more than what we have - a room where our drunkard neighbour knocks on the wall at our most private moments. Maybe this is why these private moments are becoming less and less but I have felt you withdrawing somewhere I can't reach you. When you live with a man you learn something every day. For me the hardest lesson is your solitude. Sometimes you come home and your face is like a closed door. It is as if you have gone inside the room of your mind and do not open to me.'

Janis was stunned. His worries about being an informer had somehow infected his relationship and caused Hilkka's sickness.

Article 58

Article 58

Remembrance of Things Past

Janis and Hilkka rarely talked about Siberia. When they did, it was to wonder about how a member of the family was doing or to mark a birthday or name day. Then, gradually they began to spend time going over their experiences.

One November evening Janis opened a bottle of Rigas Balsams and settled by Hilkka. 'Let's talk about the highs and lows of living in Siberia. For every low, we must also talk about a high point.' He poured two large measures and together the couple, little by little, were transported back in time and space.

After a brief pause, Janis started, 'One of the worst times I can remember was when a snake bit Mamma whilst she was raking hay into a stack with a three-pronged fork. Did I ever tell you about this? No. Well, it was in the meadows of the first collective farm that we worked on. Her leg turned blue and soon swelled so that it resembled a log. All the Latvians came to the house where she was carried in dreadful pain but no one could do anything to help. The nearest hospital was over sixty kilometres away and the locals said that when this happened before the person died on the way there. You can imagine how I felt. I remember hitting against the frame of the house and cursing Siberia, communism and Stalin. A Russian woman laid a hand on my shoulder. Using Stalin's name in vain, even in a foreign language, clearly was not going to help anyone.' 'You really must have been frantic,' Hilkka added.

Janis continued, 'Yes, I was. I hardly left Mamma's side for over two days and constantly mopped her forehead as the venom increased her heart rate and temperature. I am not ashamed to say this; in the dark of the night I whispered, 'Don't leave me here. Don't leave me here.' Despite the dreadful pain and the swelling Mamma obviously recovered and eventually returned to the meadow. After that, everyone was especially vigilant about looking for snakes. As you probably found, snakes would warm themselves by the wooden huts and we had to be really careful when stepping out of the door.'

Hilkka added, 'Yes, I remember the snakes. One of the worst things was going out to the small privy at night. Gripped by the worry of snakes hiding in there and hearing the cry of distant wolves I often found it difficult to finish the business that I had gone to do!' They laughed and then Janis said, 'Now your turn.' Hilkka countered with, 'First tell me about one of the highlights.'

Janis agreed to tell of a highlight and after a moment of reflection talked of the time that he and his mother were transported to the Far North via Krasnoyarsk.

'Did you see the famous Krasnoyarsk Posts when you travelled along the River Yenisei? From where we disembarked we could see them in the far distance... As no one knew when the boats were coming to take us further some of the boys, including myself, decided to explore these massive granite rock formations.

Article 58

From the top of the Posts we could see over fifty kilometres away across the vastness of Siberia. The Yenisei stretched out for what seemed eternity. I remember exploring the caves and running down the scree. Launching myself off the steep slopes and sliding on the scree as it avalanched down was one of the most exhilarating things I have done. We returned, tired, to a great uproar. The boats had arrived and we were about to be left behind as runaways. Luckily we were back just in time. Now Hilkka, it is your turn.' Janis refilled their glasses.

Hilkka started hesitantly, 'I am not sure if I have any stories that I have not told you already,' then she remembered when a family of bears arrived. 'Yes, a highlight of one summer was the arrival of a family of bears. It must have been the smell of fish that lured them and they were continually seen around the settlement. Gradually they got nearer to our hut. On one occasion, our foreman opened the front door of his hut and it hit a bear on his step. Luckily for the foreman, it sent the bear running off.'

'Near to our hut a canvas sheet had been hung up on birch poles to provide a shelter from the rain. In the middle of this there was a large table used for cleaning and salting the fish. One day, as I was approaching the hut I saw one of our women, Mrs. Hinkkanen, go into the shelter. Mrs. Hinkkanen was a large lady and had been fearless and hard working. Then there was a huge scream and a roar. Out ran Mrs. Hinkkanen closely followed by a bear with a table on its back. The bear must have crept in to eat the fish intestines that were under the table and then was disturbed by Mrs. Hinkkanen's return. I was unsure which of the two, Mrs. Hinkkanen or the bear, were the most scared.'

Janis laughed with the image of the bear running off with a table on its back and then said, 'Yes, I remember how we were troubled once with the bears. They pulled the nets from the lake and tore them up to get to any fish that they found. They proved to be a real nuisance until our Brigade acquired Leo. I think that I have already told you about our dog. Leo was so lion-like in his fearlessness. With a shout of 'Leo – bear', the dog would chase in a circle around the huts and scare away any bear that came too close. For some reason he disappeared one day never to return or you would have met him.'

Janis continued the recollections, 'Do you remember how in mid-August the famous Teruhanska herring would arrive? We caught them in such abundance. Small and fat, I remember how we used to eat them raw. Hmm. Did you know that many years before, people used to arrive just for this seasonal treat? Back then the fishermen would return home with their catch and earn a small fortune. Of course, we were paid a pittance.' Hilkka countered with, 'Yes, Jani, I do remember how tasty they were but do you remember the effect that they had?' Both laughed at the memories of having to rush often to the outside privy.

Hilkka thought for a while and then said, 'One of the worst things was going to school. In the first village we settled in there was a school and my sisters and I had to attend. At first we had to sit all day listening to a teacher in a language that we did not understand. When we began to learn the language, all we heard was how wonderful the Soviet Union is. The worst of it though, was always remembering how much fun we used to have at school in Finland. There was always singing and I loved best our art classes. In our Siberian school we didn't have paper let alone paint.' Janis added, 'I went to a school of a different kind where the teacher was a bear and the headmaster was the Purga.'

Now that Janis had started, thoughts from Siberia flooded back. He recounted the time that he and his friend Harijs were starting out on their careers as hunters. 'I remember Harijs and I saw the local boys in the village one day and they were laughing at us and then they pointed their fingers and whispered. I demanded to know what they were laughing about and we were ready to fight when the boys kept on sniggering. Then they told us that we were trying to catch polar grouse using ermine traps. Harijs and I laughed and the tension suddenly eased. Our meeting concluded in the normal way of a big wrestling match that ended only when everyone was out of breath.

'The next day, two of the Russian boys took pity on us and showed how to set the traps to catch ermine. This involved forming a hill through which ran a tunnel with bait at one end.'

Janis suddenly sat upright and he could feel his heart beat fast. Quietly he said to Hilkka, 'I have just realised that I never really thanked Harijs for saving my life when the Purga blew up.'

After making love, Janis realised that talking of Siberia had lifted some of Hilkka's sadness and that they had had one of the best evenings in quite a while. Then he thought, 'But of course we really didn't talk of the worst moments. I never mentioned Velichko and there might be things that Hilkka is keeping from me. I did not talk about the constant aches and pains from sleeping on boards and how we survived winter by being either hyper alert or in state of near delirium when the hunger became too great.' Nevertheless as Janis moved from being awake to the borders of sleep he thought for the first time about voluntarily returning to Siberia.

Harvest Time 1941

Recalling images and incidents in Siberia became more persistent for Janis. One evening he decided not to read a book but instead sat back and actively thought about the possibility of returning.

Janis asked himself, 'Had it all been bad?' and answered, 'No, mid-Siberia has real beauty. Could I live there? Possibly?' Janis' thoughts went back to the harvest time in Kulichki village.

Towards the end of summer in 1941 the harvest began. Everyone was pressed harder than before. The work in the fields was endless and Janis and his mother were there from morning to night. The fields were huge and the days were long and hot. There was no shade and the only relief was being able to have a bucket of water at the end of the day from the well to wash off the sweat and dust.

After harvesting, the field-workers scavenged to find out what was left after the combine had been used. Gathering the fallen grain in this way was considered to be stealing and so they had to do this early in the morning or late into the evening. Janis was quickly picking up Russian and with his newly found linguistic skills was able to borrow a small hand mill from a neighbour to grind the grain into course grit that could be used for porridge.

After the harvesting and threshing came the winnowing. The Latvian ladies soon learnt from the locals to take small bags with them. At the end of the day these bags were filled and hidden upon their person but where to hide the bags was tricky as the lame old warehouse supervisor especially enjoyed his checking duties. Bags that were concealed about the waist or between the breasts were easily found. Sonja used to bring the contraband grain back in her boots and Janis was proud of his mother for her daring.

In September the weather became warm and wet, ideal for mushrooms. Together with his mother, some of the Latvian women and most of the locals, Janis headed to the forest to pick the season's bounty.

It was quite a journey by horse and cart to the area that was known to be a good 'hunting' area. Soon the large group split into smaller groups. Janis, his mother and two other ladies, Ilga and Inta, kept together as, heads down, they started to look for the biggest and best mushrooms. Occasionally Janis looked up and observed his fellow gatherers. He was satisfied. This reminded him of happy times in Latvia when his family left the city and headed out into the outlying forests to pick mushrooms. Just as then, he recalled how quiet the forest was. The mossy ground and berry-laden bushes absorbed the sound. Not even birdsong was heard.

The forest floor was festooned with fungi but Janis found that most were infested with worms and he and his mother had to carefully select the good ones to put in their basket. So, it was quite a time before their baskets were full. Janis looked up and saw his mother and in the distance was Inta but there was no sign of Ilga.

They all shouted for Ilga but the closeness of the trees and the soundproofing of the forest floor must have muffled their voices for there was no reply.

Becoming increasingly concerned, the small group waited a while and then decided to find the clearing from where they had started. 'Maybe Ilga has found her way back to the waiting horse and carts?' but Janis did not sound convincing. In deciding to return to the clearing Janis saw a look of concern pass over their faces. He realised that they felt lost. Inta pointed in a direction that she thought they needed to go and Janis tried to look confident when he pointed in almost the opposite direction. He knew that getting the direction wrong could be fatal. The taiga stretched for a thousand kilometres and they might travel a day without coming across a path.

Janis was quietly relieved when his suggested direction took them back to the horse and carts. However, the relief was only temporary as Ilga was not there. Janis unhitched one of the horses and got on its woolly Siberian back. 'Janis be careful,' his mother urged. He then rode into the forest and soon started to call Ilga's name. Janis travelled for about thirty minutes into the deep and incredibly disorientating forest, then he heard a shout. He soon discovered Ilga in tears. Janis dismounted and Ilga hugged him and wept for a while. To his surprise, Janis found that there was an erotic charge to being hugged by a woman whose life he had just saved. He helped Ilga up onto the horse's back and together they trusted their woolly steed to retrace its steps.

When they got back to the clearing Sonja gave a cry of relief. She hugged Janis and Ilga and for a short while Janis basked in the warm glow of hero worship.

The locals had already left with their heaps and heaps of mushrooms. Janis wondered how they had managed to find so many good ones so quickly. It turned out that they picked even those full of worms. He was told later that this was not a Sunday afternoon picnic for them. Mushrooms were vital to help them get through the winter and the worms would come out with salting. 'It is strange,' thought Janis, 'that they don't pick any of the really tasty mushrooms that Mamma and I think are the best.' He later discovered that the locals thought that this type were poisonous.

On the journey back it started to rain quite hard. Janis was keen to spur the horse on quickly before the passengers were completely soaked but it would suddenly stop for no apparent reason. The small woolly bundle moved at its own pace. Janis was advised to speak to the animal in Russian. Janis' gentle urging in fledgling Russian did little to alter the horse's behaviour. On another occasion, and out of the earshot of ladies, he let go of his newly acquired vocabulary of Russian expletives. The horse immediately quickened its pace and behaved impeccably. 'Clearly,' Janis thought 'the expletives normally precede a beating if it doesn't behave.'

Janis enjoyed his jobs with the horse, especially that of transporting the grain back to the kilns. On the way he would race the other carts back and often the young riders could be heard whooping like cowboys as they urged the steed to go faster. When they weren't running the pony express to get the mail through, the boys, led by Janis, were hunting and gathering for berries. It filled them with a sense of pride that they were able to bring food home for the table.

In the autumn the farm duties changed and everyone had to congregate around the administration building in the morning to await instructions. Often these orders, once given, were soon changed. Janis' main duty was to attend to the wood-fired boiler that powered the threshing machine. This involved maintaining the pressure within set limits by feeding the fire with plentiful amounts of birch and aspen logs that continually had to be chopped. With all this physical work Janis became quite muscular.

Janis realised that he had been thinking about the autumn in Siberia for some time and had become absorbed by his memories. He sat back in his chair, looked around the cramped room and focused on Hilkka who sat sketching at the table adding the finishing touches to her recollected images of Siberia. Janis was struck by the thought that Hilkka partly resided there now. He looked past her and at the thinly curtained windows. He thought about what was outside and compared the compacted mud and scrubby grass to the wide-open space of Siberia with its big, blue, lark-filled skies. Janis remembered the village that he first stayed in. The inhabitants did not have gardens and it was clear why not. For a brief period flowers were everywhere.

Janis recalled the times in Riga when he used to go to church with his class for the harvest festival. He had enjoyed seeing the wheat stacked up in the nave together with the baskets of fruit for which they gave thanks. He began to wonder whether he had just dreamt of these happy harvests. In mid-Siberia pocketing a potato was a crime against the Soviet state. 'But,' Janis thought, 'that is not Siberia's fault. The ground is fertile and the only reason for starvation is the inefficient collective farm system.'

Janis finished his recollections with the thought, 'When Stalin has put his general's hat on the peg for the last time maybe we could think of moving, as a family, to mid-Siberia?'

Death of Stalin

In February 1953 Janis walked into the Ministry of the Interior and pushed a bell for attention. After a short while a panel opened in the wall like a small mean mouth in a bland uncaring face. A voice asked, 'What is your business?' When Janis said, 'I want to apply to return to exile in Siberia,' the voice simply asked for a name and personal code.

Janis sat in the foyer of the Ministry for hours and this gave him the opportunity to think about the conversation he had the night before with Ginta when he told her of his intention to return to Siberia. She had not been against the idea and indeed was pleased that Janis would be able to look after their mother. The letters from her made it clear that a return to Latvia was not possible. Janis had asked Ginta how she would cope if he left Riga, possibly never to return. He recalled her reply, 'Jani, of course I would like you to be here close to me but you have Hilkka to care about and I don't think living in Riga is doing her much good. Of course Siberia is not ideal but her family is there and this makes such a difference. Don't worry about me... And I have some good news to report. I am pregnant!' Janis eyes opened wide and he took a deep breath before he said, 'But....' Ginta cut him short, 'You've probably guessed. I am in a relationship with the Director of the Opera House, Mikhail. We have kept this quiet because he is a very prominent person and I am, after all, the same as you, 'a child of an enemy of the people'. I haven't wanted to endanger his career but soon we are going to get married. I think that everything will be well. We are lucky as the ballet is a major Soviet project. It shows that Russia is civilised. I don't think that we will be denounced. And anyway, Uncle Stalin is not going to live forever.'

The clock on the wall tick-tocked its way to noon and on into the afternoon. Eventually Janis was escorted to a room on the fourth floor. Sitting behind an enormous desk, which despite its size seemed to strain under the weight of documents, was a man with a large black patch over one eye that dominated his face. 'What do you want?' the patch asked abruptly. Janis expanded on his earlier request, 'I am a child of an enemy of the people who was deported and allowed to return to my home in Riga. Now I wish to move, together with my wife, to Igarka in the far north of Siberia to be with my mother.' The patch's response was curt, 'You think that the Ministry of the Interior is some sort of travel agency? That is not how the Soviet system works.' Janis felt the need rising in him to poke the man's other eye out. Instead, he managed to quell his anger and said, 'I am prepared to work for the Soviet Union in any capacity that is wanted. I am good with an axe. Siberia needs men like me.' Janis was surprised when the patch said, 'Siberia needs fit men. You are an invalid.' There was a long silence and Janis wondered whether he had been dismissed when the patch grunted, 'Come back in a week's time.' Janis wondered whether the patch had just realised that a potential problem could be exported.

Janis returned the next week and was told by the hidden face in the reception that the man he needed to see was busy and to come back in a week's time. He duly returned in the full expectation that he could be yo-yoing in and out of this office quite regularly. To his surprise, he was informed that the patch was in and after a long wait Janis was escorted once again to him. He stood in front of the burdened desk. After a while the patch said, 'Granted. You and your wife are to be relocated to Igarka and you both have permission to travel after the 5th March. You must report to the Regional Commander's office by 20th March. You have two choices. You can pay for the trip or travel as *zeks*, prisoners.' Janis thought about his first meeting with the urki and immediately said, 'We will pay,' although he had no money.

Janis returned immediately to see Hilkka and gave her the news. He was surprised with her reaction, 'Oh, Jani, I am happy. I cannot believe it but I am. I can't wait to see my sisters and father. I am so looking forward to seeing your mother. Maybe in the summer you can start to play your harmonica again and we can sing our folksongs. I am not forgetting the cold and the rain, the mud, the bed bugs and the moskas but today I am happy'. Janis did not immediately tell Hilkka that they had to find the money from somewhere for their return or they would be separated and transported as *zeks*.

When Janis told Ginta later in the day about gaining permission to return he also told her that he had to find the money to pay for the train fare and subsistence to Igarka. Ginta said, 'Mamma is going to need your help and it is very good of you to return. I will find the money. I will ask Mikhail. He will be able to help.'

Before the departure date Janis gave in his notice at the hospital. The same day that he did this he was passed a piece of paper whilst waiting at the tram stop. His heart sank. He had hoped to just disappear without letting the NKVD know where he had gone.

At the prescribed date and time Janis reported to his 'clerk'. He was asked the usual question, 'What do you have to report?' The clerk feigned surprised when he replied, 'Nothing.' Before he was able to say anything more, Janis added, 'I quit, resign, I am off. I am returning to Siberia.' The clerk said, 'I have been informed of such, but let me inform you, my little informer friend, you do not resign from the NKVD. I will let this 'nothing to report' incident go this time, but your details are being forwarded to my closest friends in Igarka. Expect a call.' With that, Janis was dismissed.

Late on in the morning of 5th March 1953, Janis went to buy his tickets to Moscow. The plan was to leave on 7th March and when they arrived in Moscow, they would buy their onward leg to Igarka.

As he walked towards the station Janis looked at the temporary wooden bridge that replaced the one destroyed in the war. He could see that preparations were being made to create a new one and this seemed to sum up for him hope and history. He thought, 'There is hope here; there is new life and one that might be good for Ginta's child. But it is not for me. Riga is no longer home and has never been for

Hilkka.' Now he felt that he was about to cross a bridge and never look back.

Janis carried on walking but before he had even reached the station he could hear funereal music coming from the loudspeakers. Shortly, a large group gathered waiting for an announcement. The loudspeakers crackled and a serious-sounding voice started to speak, 'Dear Comrades and Friends. The Central Committee of the Communist Party of the Soviet Union.... announces with profound sorrow that Joseph Vissarionovich Stalin, chairman of the USSR Council of Ministers and the secretary of the Central Committee of the Communist Party of the Soviet Union, has died after a grave illness. The heart of Lenin's comrade-in-arms and the inspired continuer of Lenin's cause, the wise leader and teacher of the Communist Party and the Soviet people, has stopped beating.... the immortal name of Stalin will live for ever in the hearts of the Soviet people and all progressive mankind. Long live the great, all-conquering teachings of Marx, Engels, Lenin and Stalin.'

The news of Stalin's death was received in silence and then many started to weep. Some became uncontrollable.

Janis was surprised. There had been no news that Stalin was unwell or that his health had declined. But he did not share the onlookers' grief. He knew that he could not rejoice in public but inside he smiled. His thoughts turned to his mother, the journey he was about to make and the possibility of an improved life. He hurried back to see Hilkka.

The news of Stalin's death had beaten his return and when Janis entered his building he found Oswalds on the staircase. Oswalds had hardly talked to Janis in the past. Now he said, 'This is terrible news. What shall we do? Tell me comrade, how can I send flowers to the funeral?' Janis was not sure if Oswalds was being ironic and so he said nothing and pushed by him to enter his own room. Hilkka had already heard of the news that was broadcast over the radio of Oswalds' daughter. 'Maybe now', Hilkka said, 'there is the possibility of some normality.'

A little later in the day Ginta returned home. Janis went into her attic and noticed that she had been crying. 'Ginta, I am surprised...' He did not say anything more as Ginta cut in, 'Jani, yes I have been crying about the death of a great man. Not the one that you think. I heard that Sergei Prokofiev has also died today. I will never forget dancing in his Cinderella.'

March 8ᵗʰ 1953 – Stalin's Farewell

Janis began to wonder whether Hilkka would ever wake from her afternoon slumber. He was beginning to get restless but decided to let his wife sleep on.

Janis' thoughts went back to their wedding day and to the speech that Pauli had given. He recalled the time that Pauli had talked to him about suffering, 'Pauli held out the promise of me becoming a man if I bore my suffering with the right attitude.' Janis remembered the 'clerk's' last few words to him and concluded, 'But being the NKVD's little helper probably means that I have failed again.'

Janis returned to the idea of life being a tapestry and he being part of its intricate and interrelated thread. He then thought, 'If I have not created the pattern, who has? Can I truly say that Stalin has drawn the bigger picture? Possibly? It would be comforting to put this ugly scene down to the act of one man. But no, surely one man, however powerful, could not have done this alone?

'It is certainly true that I have suffered but who is responsible?' Janis mused. He thought about all the people whom he had seen en route to Moscow, flooding in to mourn the departed leader. In the stillness of the room he wondered whether each person carried his or her own share of guilt. 'I have been tested physically and morally and found to be wanting. Are we not all responsible for the lunacy that is going on in Russia and consequently for our individual fates too?' he pondered.

Janis suddenly thought, 'The future is not being created by one man, it comes from a myriad of conversations and the millions of daily decisions taken by everyone. If everyone wakes up tomorrow thinking, like Pauli, that there is a better future, how different the world would be.'

Janis felt a wave of optimism pass through him and thought, 'Could revolution be as easy as this; simply everyone changing the conversation? Instead of saying 'yes' they would say 'no'.'

The positive feeling that Janis generated quickly evaporated as he thought of the times that he could have said 'no'. Mostly saying such risked a punishment of sorts, possibly a kick, the edge of a rifle butt or something far worse. Then he thought, 'Most people simply repeat stories that they hear rather than make new ones. Stalin and his henchmen told the main story and everyone repeated this.' Janis realised that with the death of Stalin, the propaganda machine would continue to work and that nothing much would change.

Janis tried to shake off thoughts of Stalin by thinking of their anticipated homecoming. One of the things that Pauli had said to Janis after the accident now came back to him. He could almost hear Pauli's voice, 'The crowning experience of all, for the homecoming man, is the wonderful feeling that, after all that he has suffered, there is nothing to fear any more –

except God.' Janis shuddered. He had lost most of his fear but not of the meeting with God at which he would have to explain his killing of Velichko.

Janis was relieved when Hilkka stirred from her afternoon snooze. He went over and kissed her and said, 'Let's see if we can find something to eat then take a look at what is happening.' Hilkka said, 'Yes, let's,' then got up, quickly slipped on her dress, smoothed out the rumples and plumped her hair. Once they had donned their winter coats they were ready to leave.

Janis and Hilkka went down the stairs and past the reception of the hotel. From behind the closed panel they could hear noises of food being prepared and could smell something that seemed to be a combination of boiled cabbage and old handkerchiefs.

Leaving the hotel Janis and Hilkka both hitched up their coat collars to keep out the chill and wet snow that was falling. It was still the afternoon but the heavy sky meant that the streetlights reflected on the wet pavements and puddles in the road. Janis asked Hilkka, 'Shall we just go with the flow and see where the crowd takes us?' She replied, 'Why not? Maybe they all know something we don't and they are all going to a good restaurant that is open to all.' Janis added, 'Yes, good and cheap.'

With food on their minds, Janis and Hilkka made their way back towards the station. A constant stream of people continued to head from there towards the city centre. Around the station were a few cafes and restaurants. The cafes had large queues outside and the restaurants all had a *shveicar,* doorman whose job it was to refuse entry to almost everybody. The couple decided that there must be quieter places to eat further away from the station. They consoled themselves with the fact that, if all else failed, they still had the remnants of a loaf of bread that they had brought with them and the bottle of Rigas Balsams.

Janis and Hilkka walked along Mira Prospekts without any real purpose. They had no intention of seeing the body of Stalin as he lay in state but for a while they thought that they would go with the stream of people heading towards the centre. 'After all', Janis said to Hilkka, 'this is a historical occasion and marks the beginning of a better life for us.'

Janis was conscious that he had been in Moscow once before but had paid little attention to the city as he had been focused on getting back to Riga. Now with nothing more than a few pangs of hunger to contend with he had time to look at Moscow with fresh eyes. He talked to Hilkka about his impressions, 'Look how wide Mira Prospekts is and the trams and trolley buses are modern and frequent.' Hilkka replied quickly, 'So it should be, this is the capital of the Holy Russian Empire.' They walked on and commented on how some of the houses seemed freshly painted. They especially liked the pink ones with white plaster columns. They noted how many cars there were and how well dressed everyone looked. Janis and Hilkka were still conditioned by the terrible clothes that they wore through the severest of winters. Now anyone wearing proper winter clothes with fur hats and collars was considered to be well-dressed. 'Well-dressed yes, but everyone is dressed the same, all in black' Hilkka remarked. 'Of course, we are at a funeral,' Janis added, but also knew that this was the everyday clothing for Muscovites.

Gradually the crowd swelled and when they reached Bolshoi Sukharevskiy Street they had to turn in as trucks barred the way ahead.

Bolshoi Sukharevskiy Street was lined with soldiers and trucks. After a few hundred metres the pace of the pedestrians slowed and Janis found that they were in a wide queue of sorts. They waited for a short while for the pace to pick up again and when it did not they thought of turning around and retracing their steps. The soldiers and trucks prevented them stepping off the wide pavement and when they looked back there was a deep crowd behind them. Janis feared the Russian curses that pushing through would entail. He asked the woman next to him what she was queuing for and was surprised by her reaction, as she spat out, 'Are you stupid! We are going to see Comrade Stalin in the House of Unions.' Janis turned towards Hilkka and suggested, 'Shall we just go with the crowd?' 'Why not, we haven't much else to do,' she replied.

Janis looked at the soldiers who effectively prevented Hilkka and him from turning around and thought, 'They are part of the Russian Army that deported me. This same army killed Latvian men and raped the women a hundred years before in the time of Peter the Great. It's the same army that shot Latvians under the order of Tsar Nicolas II after the revolution of 1905. It's the same Russian army that invited themselves in to Latvia in 1939. For all that, they all look incredibly sad and miserable.'

There was temporary relief from being tightly packed when the queue emptied into Tvestnoy Boulevard next to Trubnaya Square. The couple readjusted their clothing and looked into the large enclosed square on the other side of the boulevard, which a row of army lorries prevented people from entering. As they passed other roads, hundreds of people were being disgorged into the tributary that Janis and Hilkka were slowly moving along. The flow was one way. 'Not even a human salmon could swim against that current,' Janis remarked. They resigned themselves to walking down the side of the square and then planned to retrace their steps to their hotel at the other end. They continued with the human tide that inexorably moved forward.

'To think that in two days' time we'll be off again on our journey, I can hardly wait to see Mamma's face. Pauli will be overjoyed to see you,' Janis whispered. 'Yes and I can't wait to give my sisters the lovely blouses that I've made for them,' said Hilkka.

Janis stopped his musing when suddenly the crowd became uncomfortably squashed together. Janis looked at the women next to him in a big coat and black scarf over her head. He was going to say something like, 'Why so close?' when he realised that everyone was intensely packed in.

Then, Janis saw that they were heading towards a bottleneck created by a line of army trucks. With a sudden sense of foreboding he gripped Hilkka's hand tightly and said, 'We must get out from here.' Janis tried to turn around but in that instant a hidden tentacle increased its grip and he was prevented. Janis realised that if he stopped putting one foot in front of another he would be borne along by the crowd or slip beneath the feet of others. Janis and Hilkka found that they were being marched by the crowd, tiny step by tiny step, towards the trucks. With each step the pressure built on their ribs. With rising panic, Janis dug his heels in and tried to push back, but the surge was unstoppable.

Janis could see that the crowd was being caught between the trucks. 'Get the trucks out of the way,' people ahead could barely utter the words for lack of breath. 'I have no orders', shouted back a young, bewildered soldier.

Suddenly, Janis was filled with a savage hatred for everything that had given birth to the mentality of 'I have no orders', and thought, 'Suspicion and fear has paralysed everyone.'

People were being crushed against the trucks in almost eerie silence. Janis thought of the body that lay cold in the House of Unions. To him it was clear that, from his coffin, Stalin, was still dealing out death at random to his subjects.

Still the trucks did not move. Janis tried to shout but could only take rabbit-like breaths.

The breath of thousands of people jammed next to each other rose up like a white cloud. Janis felt his hand slip away from that of his wife and could not force his way back to her. He called out in what only amounted to a whisper, 'Hilkka.'

Postscript

People were killed on Moscow's Trubnaya Square during the lying in state of Joseph Stalin. Although the exact body count is still classified information it is estimated that between several hundred and three thousand people suffocated to death in the huge crowds that came to mourn the death of the Soviet leader.

Article 58

Appendix

Instructions of the Soviet Deputy Commissar for
Public Security, Serov

1. - INSTRUCTIONS
Regarding the Procedure for carrying out the
Deportation of Anti-Soviet Elements from
Lithuania, Latvia and Estonia

Strictly Secret

1. GENERAL SITUATION
The deportation of anti-Soviet elements from the
Baltic Republics is a task of great political
importance. Its successful execution depends upon
the extent to which the district 'troikas' [A body
consisting of three members] and operative
headquarters are capable of carefully working out a
plan for implementing the operations and for
anticipating everything indispensable. Moreover, care
must be taken that the operations are carried out
without disturbance and panic, so as not to permit
any demonstrations and other troubles not only on
the part of those deported, but also on the part of a
certain section of the surrounding population hostile
to the Soviet administration.

Instructions as to the procedure for conducting the
operations are given below. They should be adhered
to, but in individual cases the collaborators engaged

in carrying out the operations shall take into account the special character of the concrete conditions of such operations and, in order correctly to appraise the situation, may and must adopt other decisions directed to the same end, viz., to fulfill the task entrusted to them without noise and panic.

2. PROCEDURE OF INSTRUCTING

The instructing of operative groups by the district troika shall be done as speedily as possible on the day before the beginning of the operations, taking into consideration the time necessary for travelling to the scene of the operations.

The district troika shall previously prepare the necessary transport for the conveyance of the operative groups in the village to the scene of the operations. On the question of allocating the necessary number of motorcars and wagons for transport, the district troikas shall consult the leaders of the Soviet party organised on the spot.

Premises for the issue of instructions must be carefully prepared in advance, and the capacity, exits and entrances and possibility of intrusion by strangers must be considered.

Whilst instructions are being issued the building must be securely guarded by operative workers.

Should anybody from among those participating in the operations fail to appear for instructions the district troika shall at once take steps to replace the absentee from a reserve which shall be provided in advance.

Article 58

Through police officers the troika shall notify those assembled of the Government's decision to deport a prescribed contingent of anti-soviet elements from the territory of the said republic or region. Moreover, they shall briefly explain what the deportees represent.

The special attention of the (local) Soviet party workers gathered for the instructions shall be drawn to the fact that the deportees are enemies of the Soviet people and that, therefore, the possibility of an armed attack on the part of the deportees cannot be excluded.

3. PROCEDURE FOR ACQUISITION OF DOCUMENTS
After the general instructions of the operative groups, documents regarding the deportees should be issued to such groups. The deportees' personal files must be previously collected and distributed among the operative groups, by communes and villages, so that when they are being given out there shall be no delays.

After receipt of the personal files, the senior member of the operative group shall acquaint himself with the personal affairs of the families that he will have to deport. He shall, moreover, ascertain the composition of the family, the supply of essential forms for completion regarding the deportee, the supply of transport for conveyance of the deportee, and he shall receive exhaustive answers to questions not clear to him.

Simultaneously with the issuing of documents, the district troika shall explain to each senior member of the operative group where the families to be deported are situated and shall describe the route to be followed to the place of deportation. The roads to be taken by the operative personnel with the deported families to the railway station for entrainment must also be indicated. It is also essential to indicate where the reserve military groups are stationed, should it become necessary to call them out during trouble of any kind.

The possession and state of arms and ammunition of the entire operative personnel shall be checked. Weapons must be in complete battle readiness and magazine loaded, but the cartridge shall not be slipped into the rifle breach. Weapons shall be used only in the last resort, when the operative group is attacked or threatened with attack or when resistance is offered.

4. PROCEDURE FOR CARRYING OUT DEPORTATIONS

If the deportation of several families is being carried out in a settled locality, one of the operative workers shall be appointed senior as regards deportation in that village, and under his direction the operative personnel shall proceed to the villages in question.

On arrival in the villages, the operative groups shall get in touch (observing the necessary secrecy) with the local authorities: the chairman, secretary or member of the village Soviets, and shall ascertain from them the exact dwelling place of the families to be deported. After this the operative group, together with the representatives of the local authorities, who shall be appointed to make an inventory of the property, shall proceed to the dwelling of the families to be deported.

Article 58

Operations shall be begun at daybreak. Upon entering the home of the person to be deported, the senior member of the operative group shall assemble the entire family of the deportee into one room, taking all necessary precautionary measures against any possible trouble.

After the members of the family have been checked in conformity of the list, the location of those absent and the number of sick persons shall be ascertained, after which they shall be called upon to give up their weapons. Irrespective of whether or not any weapons are delivered, the deportee shall be personally searched and then the entire premises shall be searched in order to discover hidden weapons.

During the search of the premises, the members of the operative group shall be appointed to keep watch over the deportees.

Should the search disclose hidden weapons in small quantities, these shall be collected by the operative group and distributed among them. If many weapons are discovered, they shall be piled into the wagons or motorcar that has brought the operative group, after any ammunition in them has been removed. Ammunition shall be packed and loaded together with rifles.

If necessary, a convoy for transporting the weapons shall be mobilised with an adequate guard.

In the event of the discovery of weapons, counter-revolutionary pamphlets, literature, foreign currency, large quantities of valuables, etc., a brief report of the search shall be drawn up on the spot, wherein the hidden weapons or counter-revolutionary literature shall be indicated. If there is any armed resistance, the question of the necessity of arresting the parties showing such armed resistance and of sending them to the district branch of the People's Commissariat of Public Security shall be decided by the district troikas.

A report shall be drawn up regarding those deportees in hiding or sick, and the representative of the Soviet party organisation shall sign this report. After completion of the search the deportees shall be notified that, by a Government decision, they will be deported to other regions of the Union. The deportees shall be permitted to take with them household necessities not exceeding 100 kilograms in weight:

1. Suit
2. Shoes
3. Underwear
4. Bedding
5. Dishes
6. Glassware
7. Kitchen utensils
8. Food – an estimated month's supply
9. Money in their possession
10. Trunk or box in which to pack articles
    It is not recommended that large items be taken.

If the contingent is deported from rural districts, they shall be allowed to take with them small agricultural stocks – axes, saws and other articles, which shall be tied together and packed separately from the other articles, so that when boarding the deportation train they may be loaded into special goods wagons.

In order not to mix them with articles belonging to others, the Christian name, patronymic and surname of the deportee and name of the village shall be written on the packed property.

When loading these articles into carts, measures shall be taken so that the deportee cannot make use of them for purposes of resistance while the column is moving along the highway.

Simultaneously with the task of loading by the operative groups, the representatives of the Soviet party organisations present at the time shall prepare an inventory of the property and the manner of its protection in conformity with the instructions received by them.

If the deportee possesses his own means of transport, his property shall be loaded into the vehicle and together with his family shall be sent to the designated place of entrainment.

If the deportees are without any means of transport, carts shall be mobilised in the village by the local authorities, as instructed by the senior member of the operative group.

All persons entering the home of the deportee during the execution of the operations or found there at the moment of these operations must be detained until the conclusion of the operations, and their relationship to the deportee shall be ascertained. This is done in order to disclose persons hiding from the police and other authorities.

After verification of the identify of the detained persons and establishment of the fact that they are persons in whom the contingent is not interested, they shall be liberated.

If the inhabitants of the village begin to gather around the deportee's home while operations are in progress, they shall be called upon to disperse to their own homes, and crowds shall not be permitted to form.

If the deportee refuses to open the door of his home, notwithstanding that he is aware that the members of the People's Commissariat of Public Security have arrived, the door must be broken down. In individual cases neighbouring operative groups carrying out operations in that locality shall be called upon to help.

The delivery of the deportees from the village to the meeting place at the railway station must be effected during daylight; care, moreover should be taken that all the assembling of every family shall not last more than two hours. In all cases throughout the operation firm and decisive action shall be taken, without the slightest excitement, noise and panic.

It is categorically forbidden to take any articles away from the deportees except weapons, counter-revolutionary literature and foreign currency, as also to make use of the food of the deportees.

All participants in the operations must be warned that they will be held legally accountable for attempts to appropriate articles belonging to the deportees.

Article 58

5. PROCEDURE FOR SEPARATION OF DEPORTEES FAMILY FROM HEAD OF THE FAMILY

In view of the fact that a large number of deportees must be arrested and distributed in special camps and that their families must process to special settlements in distant regions, it is essential that the operation of removal of both the members of the deportee's family and its head should be carried out simultaneously, without notifying them of the separation confronting them. After the domiciliary search has been carried out and the appropriate identification documents have been drawn up in the deportee's home, the operative worker shall complete the documents for the head of the family and deposit them in the latter's personal file, but the documents drawn up for the members of his family shall be deposited in the personal file of the deportee's family.

The conveyance of the entire family to the station shall, however, be effected in one vehicle and only at the station shall the head of the family be placed separately from his family in a car especially intended for heads of families.

During the assembling (of the family) in the home of the deportee the head of the family shall be warned that the personal male effects must be packed in a separate suitcase, as a sanitary inspection of the deported men will be made separately from the women and children. At the stations of entrainment, heads of families subject to arrest shall be loaded into cars especially allotted for them, which shall be indicated by operative workers appointed for that purpose.

6. PROCEDURE FOR CONVEYING PRISONERS

The assistants conveying the column of deportees in horse-carts are strictly forbidden to sit in the said carts. The assistants must follow alongside and behind the column of deportees. The senior assistant of the convoy shall from time to time go the rounds of the entire column to check the correctness of the movement.

When the column of deportees is passing through the inhabited places or when encountering passersby, the convoy must be controlled with particular care; those in charge must see that no attempts are made to escape, and no conversation of any kind shall be permitted between the deportees and the passerby.

7. PROCEDURE FOR ENTRAINMENT

At each point of entrainment a member of the operative troika and person specially appointed for that purpose shall be responsible for the entrainment.

On the day of entrainment the chief of the entrainment point, together with the chief of the deportation train and of the conveying military forces of the People's Commissariat of Internal Affairs, shall examine the railway cars provided in order to see that they are supplied with everything necessary, and the chief of the entrainment point shall agree with the chief of the deportation train on the procedure to be observed by the latter in accepting the delivery of the deportees.

Red Army men of the conveying forces of the People's Commissariat of Internal Affairs shall surround the entrainment station.

Article 58

The senior member of the operative group shall deliver to the chief of the deportation train one copy of the nominal roll of the deportees in each railway-car. The chief of the deportation train shall, in conformity with this list, call out the name of each deportee, shall carefully check every name and assign the deportee's place in the railway-car.

The deportees' effects shall be loaded into the car, together with the deportees, with the exception of the small agricultural inventory, which shall be loaded into a separate car.

The deportees shall be loaded into railway-cars as families; it is not permitted to break up a family (with the exception of heads of families subject to arrest). An estimate of twenty-five persons to a car should be observed.

After the railway-car has been filled with the necessary number of families, it shall be locked.

After the people have been taken over and placed on the deportation train, the chief of the train shall bear responsibility for all persons handed over to him and for their delivery to their destination.

After handing over the deportees the senior member of the operative group shall draw up a report on the operation carried out by him and shall address it to the chief of the district operative troika. The report shall briefly indicate the name of the deportee, whether any weapons and counter-revolutionary literature have been discovered, and also how the operation was carried out. After having placed the

Article 58

deportees on the deportation train and having submitted reports of the results of the operations thus discharged, the members of the operative group shall be considered free and shall act in accordance with the instructions of the chief of the district branch of the People's Commissariat of Public Security.

DEPUTY PEOPLE'S COMMISSAR OF PUBLIC
SECURITY OF THE USSR

*Commissar of the Public Security of the Third
Rank*

(Signed) SEROV

Article 58

Article 58

About the Author

Russell John Connor lives in Windsor, England. He first went to Latvia in 1994 as the HR Director of the newly privatised telecommunication company. Since then he has been fascinated by the survivor stories of those who were uprooted from a pleasant land and exiled to one of extremes.

In 2012, Russell was given copies of 'There Was Such a Time' by Ilmars Knagis and 'The Children of Siberia' compiled by Dzintra Geka. Knagis chronicles his life as a deportee up to the breakup of the Soviet Union. Dzintra Geka compiled seven hundred and twenty four recorded interviews with Latvian children who were deported. These books provide the raw material and inspiration for 'Article 58'.

Russell is the author of six business books, *'The Ten Commandments'*, *'It's About Time'*, *'The Future is Imagined'*, *'Building a Flourishing Organisation'*, *'Building a Flourishing Career'* and *'What Goes Zubb?'*

Lightning Source UK Ltd.
Milton Keynes UK
UKHW02f1127300718
326492UK00012B/708/P